THE HUNGRY GHOST

H. S. NORUP grew up in Denmark and has since lived in the UK, the US, Austria, Singapore and Switzerland, where she resides with her husband and two teenage sons. She has a master's degree in economics and business administration and sixteen years' experience in corporate marketing strategy and communications. When she's not writing or reading, she spends her time outdoors either skiing, hiking, walking, golfing or taking photos. Her debut novel, *The Missing Barbegazi*, which was shortlisted for the Red Dot Award and named a *Sunday Times* Book of the Year, is also available from Pushkin Children's.

THE HUNGRY GHOST

H.S. NORUP

PUSHKIN CHILDREN'S

Pushkin Press
71–75 Shelton Street
London WC2H 9JQ

The Hungry Ghost was first published in 2020 by Pushkin Press

3 5 7 9 8 6 4 2

ISBN 13: 978-1-78269-269-0

Designed and typeset by Tetragon, London
Printed and bound in the United States

www.pushkinpress.com

For my mum,
Lis Sidelmann Jørgensen (1942–1990)
Always part of my life.

—I—

You can't see the stars here in Singapore. Ghostly, dimmed spots fade in and out on a sky that's not black but a murky, yellowy grey.

"I can't see the stars today, Freja." That's what Mum always says when she's sad. Even if it's the middle of the day.

Are the stars invisible here, or is it just me?

I give up on finding a star, and slump back into the cushions on the deep window seat. The only sound in the silent house is the low hum of the air-con unit. It blasts cool air down on my shoulders. Flyaway strands of hair blow into my eyes. I think about retying my ponytail.

It's midnight, but I'm wide awake. My watch still shows the time in Denmark. Six o'clock. I don't want to set it to Singapore time yet. Perhaps I have jet lag, because it feels like my whole body is confused.

I'm not sure when yesterday ended and today began. The two have blended into one endless day, where too many things happened. I remember looking at my watch exactly

7

twenty-four hours ago, at six o'clock. That was when Aunt Astrid, Mum's sister, handed me over to Dad in Copenhagen airport, like I was a parcel being passed on.

Outside the window, tips of twigs scratch against the glass. The tree's so close I think I could jump to the nearest thick branch, if I had to escape. But where would I go?

Singapore is 10,071 kilometres away from home. The distance is almost impossible to understand. Once, with my scouting troop, we hiked thirty kilometres in one day, to get the activity badge. Even if I walked that far every single day, it would take more than eleven months to get back to Mum.

In the light from the yellowy sky, I can make out shapes in the room. My suitcase lies open on the floor, spilling a jumble of stuff I had to take out to find my pyjamas. The only other things I've unpacked are my compass and the Swiss Army knife Dad gave me last summer for my eleventh birthday.

A beanbag leans against an empty bookcase. Two framed posters hang above the bed. One is of Mount Everest and the other of a jungle waterfall. Dad might have chosen them. And only them. Everything else in the room is pink and girly. Chosen by Her. My stepmother. Clementine.

I open the window to take a closer look at the tree, because a scout should always be prepared. The hot air that streams inside is sticky and dense, making me cough. It smells like something somewhere is burning. That calms me a bit, because bonfire smoke is my favourite scent.

Cicada song and something louder—frogs or perhaps toads—sound like an orchestra during warm-up. If they're toads, then I hope they're edible, unlike the ones we have

8

in Denmark. I'll ask Dad tomorrow. It sounds like there are lots of them, and that could be handy in a survival situation.

I'm glad I have rope in my suitcase, because the thick branch is further away than I thought, and it's too risky to jump from the first floor. Below, outdoor lights are burning on the covered terrace. Part of a sun lounger is visible next to the swimming pool. Behind the pool, which isn't even fenced in, the lawn and an overturned tricycle lie in half-darkness under a row of palm trees and flowering bushes. At the back of the garden, where a high hedge blocks the view of the neighbours, something's moving.

A tall man sneaks along the hedge. He's talking. I pull the window almost closed and creep back until I'm kneeling on the floor, peeking down into the garden.

The man is near the house before he steps out of the shadow under the trees. Light from the terrace falls on his yellow hair. It's Dad! He must be on the phone again, having another business call with someone in London or New York.

I get up and lean out of the window.

"Dad," I call in a stage whisper, expecting him to look up and wave.

He doesn't. Still muttering, his arms by his sides, his hands empty, he turns and walks away from the house. He's wearing PJ bottoms and a T-shirt. No pockets. So where's his phone?

"Dad," I call again, a bit louder. He still doesn't react. Why can I hear him, when he can't hear me? And who's he talking to at this hour, if he isn't on the phone?

When Dad reaches the high hedge and changes direction again, a bright patch starts following him. It looks like a person. As they get closer to the house, I see that it's a girl

9

in a knee-length white dress. Graceful as a ballet dancer, she cranes her long neck. One thin hand—with the palm turned up—stretches towards me, in either a dance move or a plea for help.

Dad isn't talking any more, and he doesn't pay any attention to the girl. It's almost as if he doesn't know she's there. Before they emerge from the shadows, the girl pirouettes and turns away, with a swirl of waist-length dark hair.

Who is she? And what's she doing here in the middle of the night?

I get down and rummage through the suitcase to find my big torch. But when I return to the window, the girl has vanished. And so has Dad.

The stairs creak. Dad crosses the landing outside my room. If he can't sleep either, perhaps we can go downstairs and have a night-time chat. I want to ask him about the girl.

After springing across the room, I open the door and stick my head out, just as the door to the master bedroom closes. In the glow from the night light on the landing, I notice the letters again. Wooden animal letters glued to the outside of my door: a frog, a rabbit, an elephant, a jellyfish, an alligator. They spell my name: FREJA.

I remember a door with letters like these when I was little. I think there was a monkey too. But there's no M in my name, so that memory must be false.

The letters remind me that this isn't just a holiday. That this is my room. My room for the next year, in my new home, with my new happy family.

—2—

After another glance down into the empty garden, I flop onto the bed and lie on my back, drawing circles on the ceiling with the beam of my torch. I catch a small gecko in the light. Lizards, Clementine called them, when she screamed for Dad to get rid of one downstairs. This one's right above my head, hanging from its cute miniature hands and feet. Its tiny heart makes its rubbery body quiver.

"Hey Lizzie," I whisper.

Hang in there, she seems to say. Turned topsy-turvy, she dances to the wall and straight down behind the framed poster of Mount Everest.

But I'm not sure I can.

I roll myself into the duvet and try to pretend it's Mum, hugging me like she did yesterday morning. Through her sobs, she kept repeating that this was a wonderful opportunity for me. She was crying so much my cheeks were wet with her tears. I didn't cry—I never cry—but I wouldn't let go of Mum. When Aunt Astrid said it was time to leave, a nurse had to help her prise us apart.

The pretend hug isn't working.

As I roll out of the duvet, it hits the bedside table. The pink lampshade wobbles. My Swiss Army knife falls down, hitting the floor with a thwack.

The familiar smooth shape is cold when I pick it up, but quickly warms in my hand under the pillow. Remembering that I nearly lost it, my heart starts thumping. If Dad hadn't asked me to check my pockets before he hoisted my suitcase up onto the conveyor belt, they would have taken my knife at security, and that would've been a catastrophe.

Since the divorce, I've flown to London to visit Dad loads of times on my own. I've always remembered to put the knife in my suitcase. But while we were waiting in the queue at the check-in counter, Aunt Astrid and Dad had a long, hushed conversation about Mum, and that made me forget.

Aunt Astrid was winding the extra-long sleeves of her home-knitted cardigan around her thumbs, enlarging some of the holes. Sentences and bits of orange yarn fluff drifted back to where I stood behind them.

Twice she said, "Freja needs to be part of a normal, happy family," and three times: "I don't blame you, Will." She only once whispered, "Now Marianne can focus on her own healing, without having to worry about Freja," but I heard it as clearly as if she'd shouted it through a megaphone, because that's the reason I've agreed to leave home. To leave Mum. Without me there, perhaps she can stop being sad.

Thinking about Mum makes my belly ache. I get up and go back to the window to look for the mysterious girl.

Nothing stirs in the garden. But I can't wait until tomorrow to ask Dad about her.

On tiptoes, I cross the landing to the master bedroom door. At home, I'd barge into the room and cuddle up next to Mum under her duvet. But here... I raise my hand to knock, then lower it again. Because if I knock, it might not be Dad who answers.

On the way back to my room, I hurry past the other door with wooden letters. There's a whole zoo—with bears and lions and elephants and other animals, but no monkeys—spelling out Billy and Eddie.

My mind skips back to when Dad and I were sitting in the enormous plane to Singapore. He took my hand in both of his and said, "I'm so, so happy you're coming to stay with us. The twins are going to love having a big sister."

I'm sure he felt me trying to pull away, because he gripped my hand tighter. But by then there was no turning back; the doors were closed and the plane was taxiing out to the runway.

"Your shooting-star wish came true," I said.

"It really did. That was a fantastic week, wasn't it?"

I nodded.

Last summer, on our canoeing trip in the Swedish wilderness, I'd used every one of my new Swiss Army knife's thirty-two features—even the fish scaler and the hook disgorger. It had been the best holiday ever. At least, until the last evening.

After a day of paddling, we'd eaten a meal of two campfire-grilled trout I'd caught and gutted all by myself. Like the other nights, we'd been lying on our sleeping mats, between our rain-poncho bivouac and the bonfire. Dad had been telling a story from when he was young and went on mountaineering expeditions. I'd told him about the raft we'd built at scout camp. We'd made it out of old oil drums, logs and rope, to escape an imaginary wildfire. That's my favourite thing about being a scout: learning to survive.

Trillions of bright stars had been lighting up the dark-blue sky. Then one of them fell, leaving a blazing trail. Dad had told me his wish was that I'd come and live with them in Singapore. It ruined everything.

In the aeroplane seat next to me, Dad beamed, as if he'd completely forgotten I had said no. As if he didn't know I was coming with him against my will.

And here I am, on the other side of the world.

Back in bed, I try to spot Lizzie without turning on the torch. When I can't find her, I close my eyes, but it's impossible to fall asleep. My head is too full of new impressions: the enormous plane, the endless pattern of the carpeted airport corridors, palm trees and exotic flowers, and cascading water inside the air-conditioned terminal.

Outside the terminal, the air was so hot and choking that it felt like being hugged by someone sweaty you don't like. But before I could tear off my hoody, we'd jumped into a freezing cold taxi, and Dad rattled off the address.

"ECP *can*? Got jam on PIE, *lah*." The taxi driver squinted at us in the rear-view mirror.

"*Can*," Dad said. He was writing messages on his phone, like he'd been doing while we waited for our luggage and at the immigration counter.

"I didn't know you speak Chinese, Dad?"

"Chinese? Ha!" He leant towards me and whispered, "That's English. Well, Singlish. Everyone cuts all unnecessary words when they speak."

"People must be very busy, if they don't have time to speak in full sentences."

"You're right about that." He frowned and stared back down at his screen.

The driver sped up and slowed down repeatedly, tapping out a rhythm on the accelerator. It made me rock back and forth and feel slightly carsick. I rested my head against the window.

Gnarled trees spread their arms above all eight lanes of traffic. Beams from the setting sun were filtered through the web of branches.

Dad was on his phone, talking about contracts and dollars.

When we drove over a bridge, up above the crowns of the trees, an immense Ferris wheel and a skyline of weirdly shaped buildings appeared. The sky glowed orange behind them.

I sat up straight. I'd never seen anything like it. It was as if I'd time-travelled to a futuristic planet. But before I had a chance to study the buildings, they were gone, and we were on a busy road with coloured lights and throngs of people everywhere. Moments later there were fewer people and more trees—orderly lines of trees—and many high-risers, some so thin they looked like matchsticks that could easily break.

The taxi stopped on a quiet street, outside the gate to a detached two-storey house. Dad pressed a buzzer on the gate, and the front door flew open.

The twins came running outside, yelling, "Daddy, Daddy!"

After putting our suitcases down, Dad swung both of them around. They were all laughing. Clementine pulled me into an awkward side-hug, in which her chin bumped against my cheek. She asked about the trip, before she joined their group in a family hug. A happy family hug.

She freed one arm and held it towards me, waving me closer, but Eddie or Billy—I can't tell them apart—wiggled down. He picked up a toy car. When the other twin followed, the family hug dissolved. The boys chased each other into the house, running away from me. It was probably for the best.

—3—

There's a bright edge along the side of the darkening curtains, when I wake up. My watch says it's almost six o'clock, so I guess it must be noon here. I can't wait to ask Dad about the girl and what he's planned for us to explore today.

From the room next door, I can hear squeals and the quiet voice of Maya, the maid, shushing the twins. Last time I saw them, before they all moved from London to Singapore, the boys could only crawl and were too small to get into trouble. Now, they're running around, climbing up on things, falling down. I'll have to find a way to avoid them.

My trouser pockets clang when I put on my combats. They might be a bit warm for Singapore, but none of my shorts have as many useful pockets, and I need space for my compass, a map, the Swiss Army knife, my notebook and the rest of my survival kit, if I'm to go hiking with Dad.

In my very own en-suite bathroom, I wash the gunk out of my eyes. There's no point taking a shower before going hiking. Although I let the cold tap run for a while, the water stays lukewarm. Lizzie the lizard observes me from above the mirror. My hair's a bird's nest of yellow straw. When I pull it back into a ponytail, Lizzie nods in approval.

While I'm padding downstairs, I survey the big open room. On the right, the lounge—with its two white sofas, pastel-coloured cushions, and small tables with vases and flowers—looks like something from a glossy magazine. In the clinic's waiting room last week, Aunt Astrid chuckled at a page with white furniture just like this and toddlers in matching white dresses and ironed shirts, saying, "Guess they don't eat strawberry jam in that house."

Left of the staircase is the dining area and a door to the kitchen. There's one placemat at the far end of the dining table. Clementine sits at the other end. A pair of dark sunglasses on top of her head holds her shiny black hair in place. Her long red nails tap-dance on the keyboard of her laptop.

"Morning," I mumble.

"Good morning, Freja." She turns to me, smiling widely, as if she's actually happy to see me. "Did you sleep well? Are you hungry? What would you like? Toast? Yoghurt? Fruit? Orange juice?"

I shrug and nod. She saunters into the kitchen in her bare feet—they don't wear shoes indoors here, she told me last night—and brings back a tray with all the things you'd normally get in a hotel. Including strawberry jam.

"Maya prepared everything for you and the other two monkeys a while ago."

"Thanks."

"Let me just share this post," she says, while I take a slice of melon.

"Where's Dad?" I ask, when she's shut her laptop.

"Your daddy had to go to the office."

"He left?" I put the toast I've buttered down. I can't believe Dad would go to work on the first day I'm in Singapore! He told me he has the rest of the week off, so we could explore the island.

"But look at this little surprise he left for you." Clementine hands me a gift-wrapped box.

Inside is a new iPhone.

"It's all set it up with Wi-Fi and I entered your daddy's and my own numbers, before I wrapped it," Clementine says. "We'll discuss rules for how much you play on it, later."

I wish Dad had done those things. Perhaps he hasn't even bought the phone himself. Her voice seems to be coming from far away. The bite of toast grows in my mouth and doesn't want to be swallowed.

"I know your mummy didn't have... er... a chance to go shopping with you, so I bought you a few absolutely necessary staples." From one of the dining chairs, she lifts three gleaming shopping bags. "It was so much fun buying girly clothes for once..."

She begins taking things out of the bags and drapes them across the table: a white top with frills, pink cut-offs, a red swimsuit, a pale pink bikini with frilly edges and a matching sundress, a white summer dress, a dress with pink dots, and two pairs of flip-flops—pink and red.

"I couldn't decide, so I took both," she says with a giggle. Both pairs have heel straps, like the ones for small kids.

Last time I wore a dress, I was in third grade. It was at Aunt Astrid and Uncle Paul's anniversary. Mum only noticed

I wore shorts underneath the skirt when I was playing tag with my cousins on the dance floor. It's one of the times I remember hearing her laugh a real belly laugh.

I know I should be grateful, and I'm trying to smile, but I can't imagine ever wearing any of it. Frilly and white clothes are utterly useless in survival situations. And there's an overall lack of pockets. Mum wouldn't have bought me these kinds of clothes.

I push the thought away, because she didn't buy the clothes I'm wearing now. Aunt Astrid did.

I swallow. It feels like there's still a lump of toast stuck in my throat.

"I suppose this isn't exactly your style, so I also found these for you." Clementine extracts three plain T-shirts and two pairs of combat shorts. One pair is light brown, and the other is my favourite shade of olive green. Both have flowery embroidery on their side pockets, which are so big they make up for the decorations. I want to put the olive ones on right away.

"Thank you," I say, pulling the shorts towards me and feeling the soft cotton of the T-shirts. The red swimsuit turns over as I pull. It has a small zipped pocket on the back—large enough for my Swiss Army knife.

Mum's far away, and Dad isn't here. Clementine is. For a moment, I want to hug her. If I'm not careful, I'm going to end up liking Clementine. Her smile is so big and obvious with that red lipstick, as if she wants to infect everyone with her own happiness. As if it were easy to make other people happy.

—4—

After the twins have taken their nap, we walk to the Botanic Gardens. Clementine wants us out of the house while the pest control men are fumigating. They begin "fogging", as she calls it, before we've left.

"Can the other insects survive?" I ask. The whole garden is already hidden under a mosquito-killing mist. "Beetles and bees are really important."

"It's more important that we don't get dengue fever. Last year there was an outbreak in our area." Clementine hurries away from the house and the foul-smelling, poisoned air.

The Botanic Gardens are beautiful. Plants in hues of lush green, with colourful explosions of exotic flowers, line the pathways. Tourists flock around statues and take selfies in front of water fountains. They waddle through themed areas with signs describing the flora in great detail. Hordes of men in yellow wellies rake and sweep, grooming the gardens. It's all very impressive, but it has nothing to do with the kind of wilderness I like. I guess that's going to be hard to find here in Singapore.

We feed fish and terrapins in one of the lakes. Every time a small turtle head pops out of the water to gobble one of the pellets they've thrown, the twins giggle. Their shiny black hair stands up at the back. It sways when they rock the double stroller back and forth. I'm glad Clementine keeps them strapped in.

On the way back, we pass a thicket of mangrove trees. Countless roots fan out around their trunks and plunge into the swampy bank of the lake. Half-hidden behind this natural shelter, a huge monitor lizard sweeps its metre-long tail over the ground, right next to the path. Clementine walks faster, but I stay a moment to watch it scrape in the dirt, searching for insects and worms. It looks prehistoric, like a dinosaur who forgot to die out.

The mist and the stink are gone when we return to the house, but Clementine wants to keep the twins indoors. I go to the pool in my new red swimsuit. It fits me perfectly and my Swiss Army knife fits perfectly in the little pocket.

I walk to the far end of the lawn, but there isn't a back entrance where the girl I saw last night might've slipped out of the garden. Thinking back, it seems strange and unreal. Why didn't Dad pay any attention to the girl, when she was so obviously trying to get him to notice her?

The long trip and the time difference had made me a bit woozy. Perhaps I dozed off while sitting in the window seat and dreamt the whole thing.

After a swim, I lie on a lounger and try to read. The sun has disappeared behind the trees. It's still hot and so humid, it feels like the air is perspiring. Although I'm not moving, beads of sweat slide down my arm. They drip from my elbow and land on a flip-flop. One of the new red ones. My swimsuit isn't dry, but it's not the least bit cold. There's no risk of catching a chill, like there would be at home.

Inside, Clementine's working on her laptop. Every now and then I hear her talking on the phone. She's arranging some kind of fancy party.

The hum of distant traffic and cicadas makes me drowsy. The muggy air is like a heavy duvet, pressing down on me. The letters in my book run together. Yawning, I put the paperback down and jump into the pool.

The water cools me and the black spots in my vision disappear. Lying back, I float, with lazy kicks of my feet, from one end of the pool to the other.

Suddenly, I have the eerie feeling that someone's watching me.

But there's no one on the terrace or inside the house behind the sliding glass doors. Nothing stirs in any of the upstairs windows either.

Standing up in the pool, I turn slowly and scan the garden.

In the dappled shade under a palm tree near the hedge, I spot a white shape.

The reflections on the water make it difficult to see clearly into the shadows, but I think it's the girl from last night.

"Hi," I call over, and I wade through the water towards her. "I'm Freja. Who're you?"

The girl just stands there. She looks like she could be my age. If I have a friend who lives around here, it will be much easier to avoid spending time with the twins.

As I pull myself out of the pool, I glance down for a split second. When I look up again, she's gone, as if by a trick of light.

"Hey, wait! D'you live next door?" I sprint across the grass and stop where she stood.

There's no sign of her. The air under the tree is chilly, as if cooled by air con. Goose pimples appear on my arms. The wet swimsuit feels cold.

I'm right by the gap in the hedge, and I press branches of a shrub aside, trying to enlarge the hole, expecting to see into the next garden.

I peer through the opening. There's a panelled wooden fence behind the hedge, and a board is missing. On the other side, water trickles in the metre-deep drain, and a car drives past. It's a side street, not a garden.

Even though I'm thin, I'd never get through the narrow gap in the fence. If the girl climbed over, then I'm impressed, because it's high and smooth, without any ridges or footholds.

She can't have vanished into thin air. There must be a trick to getting in and out of the garden. Perhaps a secret passage.

I'm going to find her so she can show me.

—5—

After putting on flip-flops and throwing the towel over my shoulders, I place my book so it prevents the gate to the street from closing. Following the fence, I half-run around the corner and find the gap. The only thing visible inside is the green of the shrub.

Back at the corner, I glance up and down the street.

The girl stands three houses away. Perhaps that's where she lives. Her long black hair hangs down over her shoulders and her white dress, which is a bit like the one Clementine has given me. I'm amazed she could climb the fence in it. When I wave, she waves back.

"Wait," I call, but she turns and runs, melting into the shadows under the trees.

I chase after her. The pavement's uneven, with driveways and trees blocking me at every few paces, so I run on the asphalt. It's useful that the flip-flops have heel straps.

Sprinting up the road, I wonder why I'm not gaining on her. I'm fast. I have long legs.

But so does she. It must be a trick of the light, but she's absurdly tall and thin.

My thighs are burning, and a stitch is stabbing under my ribs, when the street goes under a big road. I ought to turn back, but I keep running.

On the other side of the underpass, I stop and gape. It's as if I've entered a different world. Walls of lush plants tower over both sides of the street. It winds upwards, more like a country road, nestled in the dense greenery. To my right, a gravel track runs between the big road and the forest.

A little way up, the girl's standing under large palm leaves on a path that leads into the woods. She waves me towards her, before she disappears behind the plants. It's like we're playing a game.

But when I reach the path, she's gone.

"Hello. Where are you?" I duck under the long oval palm leaves and a cluster of actual, real, mini bananas. They don't look quite ripe, but it's good to know they're here if I get hungry on an expedition.

I walk up the path, peering through branches, searching for the girl.

The single trail continues under a tree with a curtain of long aerial roots hanging down from its branches. I grab a handful of the roots and try to pull downwards, testing their strength. When I hang from them in both arms, they don't give at all and easily carry my weight. That's good to know too.

"Make a sound!" I call beyond the root curtain.

Here, the undergrowth blocks the path. I want to crawl under the barrier of branches to follow her, but I'm not

26

really prepared to go hiking in a rainforest. My flip-flops and swimsuit are completely inappropriate. And although I have my Swiss Army knife in the little pocket, I can't possibly go exploring without my compass and a map.

"Hey! Come back! Can we play out here instead?" My throat rasps on the words; it's so dry.

I'm right next to a plant with upturned leaves. Near the stem, the leaves form cone-like shapes. I take hold of a leaf and tilt it towards me. There's rainwater in the cone. After smelling the water and dipping a finger in it to taste that it's fresh, I swallow the quenching mouthfuls.

A pair of eyes gleam golden under one the bushes, and a monkey scurries up a nearby palm tree.

Bird calls and cicada noise throb in my ears. Cars whoosh past on the big road. No footsteps. No answer.

Through a gap in the foliage, I spot a half-buried, cracked cement shell, covered in moss. It resembles the wreck of a small submarine, with a crumbled brick periscope. The surrounding ground's covered in dead leaves and creepers. What is it? And why is it buried here in the forest?

I wish I could take a closer look, but stepping outside the path without proper shoes wouldn't be wise. There are pythons and cobras and all kinds of venomous snakes in Singapore—I looked it up—and the poor creatures must have been driven from the city into pockets of nature like this one.

I wait for a while and keep calling, but the girl doesn't reappear.

I'm a bit disappointed. But only a bit. I hadn't expected to find a real friend on my first day here. And the girl has led me to this magical forest.

I can't wait to explore it. A place to escape to might be an even better way to avoid the twins. It's too late today, but I'll return tomorrow, wearing hiking boots and bringing the necessary equipment.

—6—

I jog back along the pavement to the house, jumping up and down the high kerbs outside gated driveways. Every few steps, I glance back over my shoulder, hoping the girl will reappear. I wish I'd seen her up-close. Apart from her white dress, the long neck and black hair, I can't describe any of her features.

Then I step in a pile of squishy gunk. My right foot slides forward. I yelp and land on my left knee, in something mushy.

Nearby, someone shouts, "Hey!"

A boy comes running to the gate I'm sitting outside.

"What're you doing?" he yells. "It's taboo to step on the offerings!"

I'm sitting in the so-called offering. It's a disgusting mixture of half-rotten mashed pumpkin and squashed banana, scattered with thin sticks.

"Sorry," I mutter, and wipe gunk off my shin and knee with a discarded paper plate.

"Stop it! You can't do that."

By the other gatepost, there's a display on a paper plate, with a slice of black-spotted pumpkin, a banana, an unlit candle and a bouquet of the long sticks. I must have stepped in one just like it.

"Sorry," I repeat. "Did you see the other girl who ran past here a little while ago?"

"No!" The boy is a bit shorter and much wider than me. He pushes his long fringe back and narrows his eyes. "It's not like I'm sitting inside the gate, counting running girls. I only noticed you because you screamed."

"I didn't scream."

"You did too."

"But do you know if a tall, thin girl with long black hair lives around here?"

"No clue," he says unhelpfully.

"And what about up there in the forest?" I ask, and point towards the underpass.

"Forest? You mean Bukit Brown?"

I shrug. With its lush plants, the forest ought to be called Bukit Green.

"Bukit Brown Cemetery," he says.

"It's a graveyard?" Perhaps the half-buried submarine is a forgotten grave. "But it's completely overgrown."

"A Chinese graveyard. It's not in use any more."

"Does anyone live there?"

He shakes his head. "*Ah Ma* has told me people used to live in a small *kampong* up there long ago."

I finish scraping the mush up on the paper plate and collecting the other bits I'd scattered. After getting up, I hold the sad remains out towards him. "What did you mean when you said it was taboo to step on your rubbish?"

"It's not rubbish! It's an offering. Don't you know anything?" The long fringe of his black hair hides his eyes. But I can hear he's rolling them, from his tone. "It's the Hungry Ghost Festival. We have to make offerings to our ancestors—feed them and burn money and so on. Otherwise their ghosts will haunt us."

Invisible spider legs tickle the back of my neck. Goose pimples race down my arms. It's utterly ridiculous, but for a moment I can't help thinking that the girl did look a bit ghostly with her white dress. "Ghosts? Really? You believe in ghosts?"

"It's clear that you don't." He rips the plate from my hand and strides back in through the gate, mumbling something about how stupid I am to go swimming, wearing red, during the seventh month.

And I think he's the stupid one, because it's the end of August. Even preschoolers know August is the eighth month.

Instead of finding a friend, I might've made an enemy. At least he should be easy to avoid.

An old Chinese woman opens the door for him. At the sight of the ruined offering, her hands fly up to cover her gaping mouth.

"*Alamak!*" she exclaims.

I duck out of sight and walk as fast as I can back to the house.

It's a bit weird that the girl led me up to the graveyard and then disappeared when I thought we were playing hide-and-seek. I'm not sure if I should be annoyed or impressed. It baffles me she could do all this in a dress. But a white summer dress doesn't make anyone a ghost.

—7—

Dad doesn't get back from the office until dinner's already on the table and it's dark outside. Maya has cooked rice with stir-fried chicken and some green vegetables I don't know. The twins are noisy, and Clementine's telling Dad about her party planning. I'm not sure he listens, because he keeps peeping at his phone. Before I can ask if he has the day off tomorrow, Clementine asks him when he's coming home from Jakarta tomorrow night.

"Jakarta? You're going to Jakarta? Isn't that far away?" I ask. Clementine said Jakarta as if he was going on a bus to the next town.

"It's a hop, skip and jump. Less than two hours' flight," Dad says without looking up from his phone. "I'm landing at twenty past eight."

So, I guess we won't be exploring Singapore tomorrow either.

Perhaps Clementine notices my disappointment, because she giggles and says, "Daddy's always travelling or working, right, boys?" as if it's a good thing. She starts singing, "*Money, money, money,*" with the twins banging their spoons on plastic plates as background.

Dad glances up at them.

He didn't use to work all the time. Or was it just that I usually only spent weekends and holidays with him? I've definitely never seen him read emails on his phone during a meal before.

When Maya has taken the twins away to get them ready for bed, I ask about the girl in the white dress and the missing board in the fence.

"Sorry, what was that?" Dad turns his phone so the screen faces downwards.

"A missing board?" Clementine asks. "I'll have to get a handyman in to fix it. I don't want anyone running around in our garden."

Dad calms her down, saying, "Don't worry. I noticed it yesterday. Not a living soul could get through that narrow gap."

"And the girl in the white dress, Dad, do you know who she is?" I'm watching him carefully. He was in the garden at the same time as the girl last night.

"I don't think any of the neighbours have children your age. I certainly haven't seen any girls with long black hair around here."

"But—" I'm about to say that I never mentioned the girl's hair, when Clementine interrupts.

"How would you know? You're never here," she says with another giggle. "But you're right. Most of the neighbours are middle-aged and have children at universities abroad. There's the Chandrans with their new baby. And Mrs Lim's grandson is living with her... Could it have been a boy?"

I can guess which boy she's talking about. "It wasn't a boy."

"Caucasian or Asian?" Clementine asks. "Or perhaps a mix, like me?"

"Maybe," I say. "How did you know she had long black hair, Dad?"

"You said that."

"I didn't."

"Then I don't know, Freja. I've had a long day at work, and I slept badly last night. Had the weirdest dreams..." He frowns at something on his phone.

"I saw her in the middle of the night too."

Dad's head snaps up, and he exchanges a look with Clementine. He turns—not just his head, but his whole body—towards me and studies me with sad eyes. "Freja..." He sighs and puts a hand on my shoulder. "Are you absolutely certain we're talking about a real girl?"

I hold his gaze while I nod. "I don't have imaginary friends any more, Dad."

"Perhaps you dreamt it," Clementine says after a long pause. "I always get muddled after sleeping outside in the heat."

"Perhaps." Chasing the girl up to the graveyard wasn't a dream, but before I can tell them about that, Dad's phone rings.

"Sorry, have to take this," he says, leaving the table.

"I'd completely forgotten about Mrs Lim's grandson." Clementine twirls her chop sticks. "He's a nice boy, Freja.

I'll talk to her to set up a play date. It'll be good for you to have a friend in the neighbourhood."

Maya calls from upstairs that the twins are ready for their story, before I can tell Clementine that I'm too old for play dates and that there's zero chance of Mrs. Lim's grandson and me ever becoming friends.

I'll just have to find the girl tomorrow. Then Clementine will know I can make my own friends, and I can convince Dad the girl isn't imaginary.

—8—

The next day I unpack. Not because I mind the mess and living out of a suitcase, which would make it easier to leave swiftly when Mum gets better. But when I come up to my room after a late breakfast, one of the twins is going through my stuff. He's sitting on my floor among a scatter of T-shirts, unwinding my climbing rope and getting himself tangled into it. One loop of the rope lies around his little neck like a noose.

"Don't touch that!" I scream.

For a moment, he just stares at me, then his face scrunches up and he lets out a siren-like wail.

Clementine comes running from downstairs, and Maya from the twins' room with a half-dressed boy on her heels.

"I don't want them in my room," I yell to Clementine, while Maya carries the sobbing twin away.

"Okay, Freja. Then make sure you close the door." Clementine starts picking up and folding the T-shirts. "Would you like me or Maya to help you unpack?"

"No. Thanks." I take the stack of T-shirts from Clementine and stomp to the pink-and-white wardrobe. Knowing exactly where each item is can be crucial in an emergency.

Behind me, Clementine says, "Let me know if you need help with anything," before she leaves, closing the door.

While I stow my things safely on top shelves and in desk drawers, Lizzie watches from the summit of Mount Everest. The sky behind the glass gives her rubbery body a blue tinge.

Splendid view from up here, she might be saying, *but why did you scream at the mini humans?*

"I don't know," I mutter.

Heavy rain drums on the roof, making it easier to ignore the whinging boys who bump against my door, and Maya saying, "No, that is Freja's room."

Late afternoon, when the rain has finally stopped, I tiptoe downstairs, carrying my hiking boots by their laces. They're still encrusted with mud from the summer camp, and I don't want to give Maya extra work. Every part of my body that isn't covered by my long-sleeved top and combat trousers has been doused with mosquito spray. My Swiss Army knife, a map and Dad's old compass—you can't rely on an app for survival—is in one pocket. Another holds my phone, my key, a snack bar and a small notebook and pen. A book of matches, the magnifying glass, a small first-aid kit and a packet of tissues are distributed among the remaining pockets. My torch hangs from one of the belt loops, my water bottle from another.

I'm prepared to enter the rainforest graveyard and search for the girl.

Clementine, Maya and the twins are at a first birthday party for "one of their little friends", who I suspect is the child of one of Clementine's friends. She wanted me to come along, as they're staying for tea, but I told her I was tired. I won't starve—Maya has prepared a plate of sandwiches for me. They'll be home late and so will Dad. It's the perfect opportunity to explore the graveyard.

The sky hangs low and grey like on a chilly autumn day, so the heat outside surprises me. It's so hot and humid my T-shirt is clammy before I've finished lacing up my hiking boots.

Making my way up the road, I carefully avoid stepping in any of the soggy offerings.

The boy calls out to me when I pass his house. He pops out of the swing chair that hangs from the ceiling of their veranda.

"Are you chasing that girl again?" he asks, while walking to the gate and brushing crumbs off his shorts. There's a smear of melted chocolate on his green polo shirt.

"I'm going to search for her. You wanna come?" I'm not sure why I ask. It's not like I want to be friends with him, but it's as if he was just sitting there waiting for me.

"To Bukit Brown? With you? No, thanks!"

My cheeks burn. He's clearly not looking for a friend or he wouldn't be so rude. "Okay. And just so you know, August is the eighth month," I say as I walk away.

From behind, the boy calls. "You shouldn't go up there. There're snakes and monkeys and wild dogs and stuff. And just so you know, it's the seventh month in the Chinese calendar. The Hungry Ghost Festival month."

Rude and a chicken. I'm still fuming when I arrive at the cemetery.

Stomping—to scare any lurking snakes off—I reach the nearest small tree and cut a long stick off with my Swiss Army knife. That ought to help ward off snakes and monkeys and dogs. I'm not sure about the "stuff".

I stop to examine the tree with the aerial roots. It's a banyan tree—I looked it up. It grows downwards, starting from a seed up in another tree, and eventually strangles its host, until no one remembers or cares what kind of tree originally stood in its place.

I haven't brought my rope, so I climb up and saw off a three-metre-long root. From a nearby branch, a black bird observes me with its blood-red eyes. When it cuckoos, I realize it's a koel. Like other cuckoos, koels lay their eggs in another bird's nest, preventing the bird babies in the host family from surviving.

Not for the first time, I wonder why Dad wants me in his happy family.

After tying the root-rope around my waist, I crawl under the dense shrubs that blocked me yesterday. Dead branches snap and brown leaves the size of placemats crackle under my feet. A musty smell of decaying wood rises from the ground. Birds call out over the high-pitched background song of cicadas. One of them sounds like a persistent car alarm. The koels cuckoo. Raindrops on the greenery glitter in the weak light. It's as if I've crossed the boundary to a magical, prehistoric world.

I can already imagine the light in Dad's eyes when I tell him about it. He'll want to find his gear right away, so we can get going. I'll lead him along the track, and he'll be nodding and saying, "Not bad." When we leave the trail and he sees this surprising wilderness, he'll forget all about his phone and work. Because this is a place for an explorer: an untamed jungle, with secrets and stories to discover.

"Hello!" I call. The sound is muted, absorbed by the rainforest. "It's me, Freja!"

Everywhere—under the branches, next to the trail—graves litter the ground. Some are crumbling bricks or greenish cement that stick out of the mass of dead leaves and tree roots and new shoots. Others are decorated with faded colourful tiles and lichen-covered Chinese statues.

I've just decided that this is my favourite place in Singapore, even if she doesn't show up, when I spot her.

Although the girl is close, I still can't quite see her features in the low light under the leaves.

"Can I help you with something? Or d'you just want to play?" I ask.

She doesn't answer, but before she turns and darts away, she glances over her shoulder. I'm certain she wants me to follow her.

She moves much slower than yesterday, weaving in and out between the trees. Tapping the ground with my stick, I crash through the undergrowth behind her. She stays ahead of me, but never tries to lose me, slowing down whenever my breathing becomes laboured.

We cross a potholed asphalt pathway and a kind of half-open shed made of metal plates. Wet clothes hang limply on a washing line between the shed and a tree. Maybe that's where she lives. Next to the shed stands a rusty bicycle and a metal structure with at least eight yellow rubber boots stuck on the rods, upside down. It looks like a fantastical tree that grows wellies.

Perhaps we're running in circles—there's no time to check my compass—but we don't pass the welly tree again.

As we're sprinting downhill, she speeds up. A stitch is prickling in my side. I have to stop. Where does she get the energy? I was going on twenty-kilometre hikes in the spring, and I'm used to racing around, exploring in the forest at home. This girl could be a marathon runner.

"Wait!" I call.

Ahead, she disappears behind a mass of green shrubs.

The ground is squelchy with rain. Cicada noise surrounds me. The bushes are dense with prickly thorns. The girl seemed to slide through them, but there's no obvious path.

I'm suddenly unsure what I'm even doing here, following a strange girl. Perhaps I should just turn around and find the way back. It's getting late. Clementine and the twins might be home soon. My clothes are clammy.

A chill runs through me. Something tickles my scalp. I brush a hand over my hair to get rid of whatever's prickling my skin, hoping it was only an insect and nothing creepy... At the last thought, I try to stop my imagination running amok. I blame Mrs Lim's grandson and his talk of ghosts.

After taking a gulp of cloying humid air, I tuck my chin down towards my chest and pull the T-shirt up to cover my face. I'm holding it in place, jutting my elbow out in front, as I push through the thorny twigs. They scratch my hands. It stings.

The girl's sitting on an overgrown gravestone. We're in a small grove, encircled by the dense shrubs. The crowns of

43

tall trees come together high above us, creating a kind of den and shutting out what little light there is. The air feels fresh and cool and hushed. I can't even hear the cicadas any more.

"Is this your secret place?" I ask. "It's perfect." This is the kind of secluded spot where you could play for hours, pretending to be in a different world.

I take a few steps forward. Her dark eyes are staring at me. The girl's hair is so long it touches the gravestone. It hangs straight down, making her neck appear extremely long and thin. Her cheekbones protrude above her sunken cheeks. Thin arms stick out of the sleeves of her dress, which is still surprisingly white, without any of the splashes of mud I have on my clothes.

One more step and I might be able to reach her.

A sudden gust of chilling wind blows into my face. I close my eyes; it's a reflex. When I open them a moment later, she's gone. None of the shrubs move, like they would if someone had just run through them.

"Hey! Come back. I'll stay further away, if you want," I call. She doesn't answer.

The cicada noise returns. Somehow the place is less magical without her, and much darker.

Why did she leave after guiding me all the way here? What is it she wants me to see?

There are other tombstones in the grove. They jut up from the ground at odd angles, half-swallowed by the rainforest. I crouch by the one she sat on, tear off creepers, and brush dead leaves away from the crumbled stone. Underneath appears the remains of an etched inscription, but I can't read it. The signs are Chinese.

I take a photo of them with my phone, using flash. I'm not sure it's clear enough, so I hold a page from my notebook against the gravestone, while I rub back and forth with my pencil, creating a silver-grey copy of the signs. One of them looks like a running, mirrored capital 'E' with legs. The other's almost crumbled away.

It's only six forty, but—unlike in Denmark, where it stays light until late, in summer—it's beginning to get dark. I turn my torch on and sweep it around the grove.

Behind the gravestone, a long, flat plate-like stone lies on the ground. It isn't covered by moss or lichen or even fallen leaves. Instead, on top of the stone, pebbles and matchstick-length twigs are laid out in a pattern.

The kind of pattern I recognize.

Morse code.

10

For a moment, the whole disappearing thing and the crumbling Chinese letters on the gravestone had me spooked. But seeing the Morse code message calms me right down. The girl's probably a fellow scout. Or a girl guide. In Denmark, we're all scouts; boys and girls aren't separated. Perhaps they are here. Maybe, if we become friends, she can bring me to meet her troop.

I feel a tingle of excitement as I light my torch on the message:

• • —   — • • —   • — • •

The letters are easy to decipher: *U* and *Y* and *Æ*. But the last letter doesn't exist here. It's a special Danish letter. And even in Danish *UYÆ* doesn't mean anything. Are there different Chinese Morse letters perhaps?

I cross the stone to study the pattern from the other side. Now it's:

■ • ■ •   ■ ■ • ■   ■ • •

CQD

Still nothing meaningful. Perhaps it's a random row of bits that have accumulated over the years. Then again, perhaps it isn't. It doesn't look random, and the tiny sticks would've been washed away by rain if they had been here earlier today. The girl must have placed the message immediately before I came into the grove.

I take a photo and copy the pattern into my notebook, trying to be as precise as I can—perhaps it isn't Morse at all but another kind of code. Afterwards, I find more pebbles and sticks and arrange them into a new pattern. I have so many questions, but until I know if she can answer, I'll only ask one:

• ■ ■   • • • •   ■ ■ ■/• ■   • ■ •   • /
■ • ■ ■   ■ ■ ■   • • ■

WHO ARE YOU

The girl is so thin, and if she lives here in the cemetery, she must be poor. I wonder if she's hungry. The snack bar in my pocket is a bit squashed and I've already broken off a bite, but I place it next to my Morse message.

"I've left food for you," I call, and hope she finds it before it's carried off by ants or monkeys.

I wish there was something else I could do for her. Something to show her I would like to be friends.

47

The creepers I pulled up around the gravestone have small yellow flowers. They make me think of the chains my friend Denise and I used to make out of daisies or dandelions when we were little. After positioning my torch, I sit down and plait the creepers into a garland. I'm out of practice, and the result isn't pretty. I don't even know if the girl will understand what it means. But it's my only idea, and I feel better after seeing the ring of tiny suns brighten the drab grey stone.

Before I leave, I mark the location on the map on my phone, giving it a small star, and jot the exact GPS coordinates down in my notebook. It's unlikely that I'll lose both my phone and my notebook.

The star on my map is far from any of the roads. I'm closest to the PIE, the Pan Island Expressway, which is south-south-west of here and must be the road I ran under. If I hold my breath, I can hear the distant hum of cars.

Clutching my stick in one hand and my torch in the other, and stopping often to check the direction on my compass, I slowly make my way out of the wilderness.

Once, I smell bonfire smoke and hear voices coming from an orange glow to my right, but I continue on as straight a course as the rainforest permits, until I reach a single trail that runs along the expressway. Here, the world is normal: three lanes of cars rush past in one direction and three rows of red brake lights snake their way in the other.

As I follow the trail back to the underpass and walk down the road, I don't need to concentrate so much, and my mind starts whirling.

The girl seems more and more strange. I'm not sure what to make of her. If only I'd taken a photo of her, so I could prove to Dad that she's real. And the graveyard... it's such a magical place, but I can't quite shake the spooky feeling that there was something else there... Something more than trees and wildlife and old gravestones. I'm half-hoping the boy will still be outside, so I can ask him about those hungry ghosts.

Just before I reach the boy's house, his grandmother comes out of the gate. She squats and lights the long sticks stuck into the pumpkin pieces. I stop to watch her set fire to a bundle of paper. The edges of the sheets smoulder before they curl around, erupting blue-yellow flames which cast uncanny shadows up on her face.

When she stands up, she looks directly at me.

"What you doing outside, girl?" she asks. "The spirits are restless."

"I'm on my way home." I walk around her and the offerings in a wide circle. There's a prickling sensation on the back of my neck and that same feeling of being watched as I had yesterday in the pool. Without glancing back, I run the rest of the way to Dad's house.

After I've showered, I can hear through the wall that Clementine and the twins are back. Maya's giving one of the boys a bath, while Clementine tries to calm the other one down. Everything's so normal.

The photo of the gravestone on my phone is blurry, so I'm glad I have the rubbing, where the sign of the running 'E' is clear. While I nibble at the sandwiches, I copy it onto a loose sheet of paper. Perhaps Clementine knows what it means.

灵

Lizzie watches my drawing from her upside-down position on the window frame, then sprints up behind the curtains, showing me how fast she can run on her four legs.

When the front door closes, I spring downstairs.

I can't wait to tell Dad about the graveyard, so I follow him into his office, on the other side of the lounge area. He's on the phone, saying "Yes" a lot while he takes his laptop out and connects it to his monitor. He sends me a brief smile and holds up a hand, indicating that I should wait.

One wall of his office is covered by a floor-to-ceiling bookcase. Between the boring law and business volumes is a shelf with books about Asia and Singapore. I read their titles: *Singapore: A Biography*, *A Life in the Colonies—from Singapore to the West Indies*, *A History of Modern Singapore*... Then I pull out an A4-sized hardback called *Singapore from the Air* and sit down on the floor to flick through aerial photos of the island. A double page shows the MacRitchie Reservoir Park, with its sprawling reservoir lakes. On the next page, both Botanic Gardens and Bukit Brown can be seen. The cemetery is even bigger than the fancy gardens.

As soon as Dad has finished talking, he comes over and gives me a big hug. I show him the aerial photo and tell him I've found the most amazing place.

"It's this wilderness, right here in the city. You need hiking boots and a compass. Have you been up there? It's literally five minutes away."

Dad shakes his head and sits back down at his desk, but I continue. I talk and talk, because that keeps his gaze focused on me. I tell him everything about the graveyard: the lush greenness, the crumbling headstones, the overgrown paths, how the rainforest has taken over the place. I tell him about everything, except what brought me there in the first place. The girl.

"You have to come. Can we go tomorrow?"

"Sure. I've taken the day off. First, though, we should get you your school uniform and books, and I need to drop this contract off at the office."

I want to keep talking to Dad, and I have an idea. "Could we make a bonfire in the garden?"

"A bonfire? In the garden?" he says, as if it's the most outrageous thing he's ever heard. As if we didn't use to make bonfires in the garden all the time, before.

"Can we? Just a small one."

"Why on earth would you want a bonfire, when it's so hot outside?"

"So we can sit and talk and watch the stars," I say, before I remember that the stars are invisible here. "Or the flames."

The laptop pings and Dad's eyes flick towards the screen. "I have to answer this. Why don't we do it another night?"

"Okay." My voice shakes, but he doesn't notice. "Does CQD mean anything to you, Dad?" I ask, in a desperate attempt to keep his attention.

"Do you mean QED? That's Latin for when you've proven something mathematically." He's still looking at the screen.

"No! C, Q, D," I say, with emphasis on each letter.

Clementine saunters into the office with a cup of tea for Dad. "Do you need help, Freja?"

I shake my head.

"Then why did you say 'CQD'?"

"That means help? In Chinese?"

"Not Chinese." Clementine chuckles. "It's an old maritime distress signal, from before SOS became the international standard."

"How do you know that?" A distress signal makes sense. Since the first time I saw her, I've had a feeling the girl needed help.

"My father was a bit of an amateur radio enthusiast. He taught me SOS and CQD and always said that even though CQD has hardly been used since the *Titanic* sank, I ought to be familiar with both." She sighs. "I miss him every single day."

I'm staring at Clementine. It's like she's becoming a different person right before my eyes. An interesting person who knows useful things, not only how to plan a party and blow-dry hair. But why didn't the girl write *Help* or *SOS*? Why use a signal that hasn't been in use for the last hundred years?

"Why do you ask?"

"Er..." I can't tell her I saw the letters in Bukit Brown, because I want the graveyard to be something Dad and I can have to ourselves.

Dad isn't even listening. His eyes are glued to his screen.

"Let's leave your daddy alone. D'you want a cup of tea, Freja? It's peppermint. Nice and soothing."

I follow her to the dining table, where she has her laptop set up next to a teapot and two cups.

"I'm doing my social media updates," she says, while she pours me a cup.

My newfound interest in her is gone again. Social media updates!

"It's so important for this party, and the sponsors—"

"Can you tell me how I pronounce this?" I interrupt and unfold the sheet of paper.

She glances at it, before she answers, "Ling. Rhymes with 'sing'."

"Ling," I repeat. "Is that a girl's name?"

"It can be," she says. "It also means 'spirit'."

53

Spirit. I shudder involuntarily.

"Are you okay, Freja? You look like you've seen a ghost."

"Yes. It's... I'm really tired. Can I take my tea upstairs?"

"Of course." She hands me the teacup. "Sleep well."

In a daze, I go up to my room. The teacup rattles on the saucer. Suddenly, it all makes sense. The way the girl moves and vanishes. Her stamina. Her clean white dress. That she appears at dusk or during the night. That she's sent me a distress signal, last used a hundred years ago. Perhaps that's when she was alive.

Staring out into the dark garden, I'm hoping to catch sight of the girl. The spirit. Ling.

I'm not scared—she seems friendly—but I'm almost certain that she's some kind of spirit. A restless spirit who needs my help.

Above me, Lizzie nods.

Why me? Is it just because I can see her? I don't have any ancestors here. No one would expect me to remember them with offerings. But perhaps she's another kind of ghost.

I'm almost asleep, when one of the twins starts crying. The sound plucks at my memory. I have an odd sense of having experienced this before—like I'm used to lying in my bed, falling asleep to the sound of crying toddlers.

Dad keeps his promise, and in the morning we drive up to my new school. It's at the top of a hill in a residential area and bordered by rainforest on two sides. The thought of excursions into the wilderness in Biology and perhaps PE lessons gives me a tickle of anticipation, but the good feeling fades at the sight of the playground. It's full of children. I'd forgotten that I'll be starting school after everyone else, because Clementine thought I needed a few days to adjust.

When a bell rings, the playground empties.

"We're not meeting my new class today," I say, before we get out of the car. I'm afraid that if we go into the class, the teacher will ask me to stay, and then Dad will go to work, and we won't make it to the cemetery. And I have to make it to the cemetery today. I have to find out if Ling has answered my message.

Last night, I was convinced she was a restless spirit, but now it's hot and sunny and difficult to believe in ghosts. Besides, who has ever heard of a ghost that sends Morse messages?

I like the school uniforms. The green of the polo shirts is a bit lighter than my favourite colour, and the lady in the shop tells me I can get combat shorts with nice big pockets instead of a skirt. Afterwards, while Dad's paying for the uniforms and books and pens and folders, I wait outside.

An expansive tarpaulin is spanned out between the school's buildings, covering a round amphitheatre. On the opposite side of the amphitheatre, a monkey appears on the topmost railing. It scuttles down the steps, across the round flat area in the centre and grasps a forgotten lunchbox. With the lunchbox under one arm, the monkey hops back to the railing, where it sits, fiddling with the snaps of the lid. It's the cutest thing ever.

When Dad comes out, I pull his sleeve and point at the monkey.

"Oh yes, the monkeys are a real pest in certain areas of Singapore," he says, before he strides to the car.

Does he mean that they are being exterminated by the pest control people, like cockroaches and mosquitoes? I'm afraid to ask.

On the way to the city, Dad's on the phone, wearing earphones. He's weaving through the traffic, overtaking swarms of scooters and small lorries with rows of workers sitting on the open carriage deck. We drive through a street lined with colourful houses, which have small shops on the ground floor with their names written in Chinese. I search for the running E sign.

"Did anyone from our family ever live here in Singapore?" I ask, as soon as Dad hangs up.

"Don't think so. One of my great-great-grandfathers worked for the foreign office somewhere in the Caribbean. Other than him, everyone in the family stayed inside the M25... Except me, of course, when I moved to Denmark."

He follows the flow of blue and yellow taxis past Buddhist and Hindu temples, a mosque and a church, into a forest of skyscrapers.

"We're almost there. I'll just drop off this contract and show you my million-dollar view."

Inside Dad's building, everything is marble and massive.

"It smells of money here, doesn't it?" he asks with a grin, and he presses the button in the lift for the 33rd floor.

I sniff, but I can only smell lemony disinfectant and my apple shampoo.

By the coffee machine in the office, a group of women croon over me. "So tall, so handsome," they say, "like her daddy" and wink at him. One of them wears skyscraper heels, which make her my height. She frowns at my combat shorts.

"She'd look so pretty in a dress," she says to Dad. Her eyes flick from my fingertips to her own long, manicured nails. "I'm sure your Clementine will take care of that."

When a thickset man with a beetroot-red nose barges through the glass doors, they all scurry back to their desks and tap away on their computers.

"Morning Mr. Henderson," the women chirp.

He steers towards us, while he mops his sweaty forehead with a large handkerchief.

"Jim, this is my daughter, Freja," Dad says. "I told you she's coming to stay with us."

The man encloses my hand in his. It feels like I'm being wrung inside a soaked tea-towel.

"Welcome to Singapore, young lady. How do you like it so far? A bit warmer here than in good old Blighty, eh? You don't mind if I borrow Daddy for a little while, do you?"

Without giving me the opportunity to answer any of his questions or tell him that I came from Denmark, Mr. Henderson strides away, calling over his shoulder, "And bring the Manila file, Will."

One of the women springs up and hands Dad a thick folder.

As soon as the door closes behind Dad, the women start talking very fast, in abrupt cryptic sentences, saying things like: "That one in Manila is *blur like sotong*," and, "*Last time*, he *catch no ball*". I guess these must be Singlish expressions.

"You can wait in there," one of them says to me. "Can I get you something to drink?"

I shake my head and follow her into an office that I know is Dad's right away. On his desk, there's a Lego model of a Volkswagen minibus, which he got for Christmas years ago. Two framed photos lean against it: one of Clementine with Billy and Eddie—all three in matching baby-blue outfits—and my latest school photo.

Through the floor-to-ceiling windows behind the desk, the view really is amazing. All the extraordinary buildings seem to be competing to be the weirdest. I decide the runners-up are a gigantic white flower, two golden-brownish hedgehog-like domes, and a row of long, flat arches. The winner in the weird-building competition, though, is a set of three tilting skyscrapers held together on top by a ginormous surfboard. The whole thing looks like the first layer in a curving house of giant cards.

I sink down on Dad's swivel chair to take it all in. The water in the bay below is almost as green as the trees in the park beyond it. The ocean is a pale blue and littered with hundreds of container ships. Only two of them are moving. From here, the rest resemble abandoned Lego bricks.

After a while, I wish I'd said yes to a drink, because I'm getting hungry. The snack bar I packed, just in case, is in my school bag in the car. I glance at the door, before I slide Dad's top drawer open, but there's nothing to eat, only pens and sticky notes.

The next drawer's empty except for two photos. They're crinkled along the edges, as if they get handled a lot. I carefully take them out. The one on top is of me as a smiling, kicking baby—Mum has the exact same photo in a frame in her bedroom.

In the other photo, we're on a beach. I'm four or five. Dad has thrown me high in the air. We're both laughing, our arms stretched towards each other. Mum's smiling at the camera. Strands of her hair are blowing across her face, but they don't hide that her eyes are smiling, too. Next to her, a little girl with blonde flyaway hair looks up from the bucket she's filling with sand. Perhaps the girl's Lulu. She's eight now and the daughter of Mum's photographer friend, who I guess took the photo. I stare at it for a long time. It's making me feel funny, like I'm falling in real life, not just in the picture.

At the sound of steps outside, I hurry to hide the photos, but it isn't Dad who opens the door. It's the woman from before. She smiles with an apology in her eyes, so I can guess she's not bringing good news.

"They're about to start a conference call with the company in Manila," she says. "I promised Will to send you home in a taxi."

In the taxi, I keep thinking about the beach photo. I don't remember that day. I don't remember seeing the snapshot. And I don't remember us ever being so happy.

—13—

Outside the house, when I'm paying with the twenty-dollar note the woman gave me, the taxi-driver says, "Never go that way at night." He points up the road towards the cemetery. His hand, in its smudged fingerless glove, shakes. "*Last time*, almost pick up a *pontianak*."

"Is that like a pangolin?" I ask. I'd love to see a pangolin in the wild.

"No. That one is a scary vampire ghost."

Another ghost story. But who's ever heard of a vampire ghost?

Until yesterday, I had never thought ghosts might be real. I still half-expect Ling will tell me she's in the local girl-guide troop, when I meet her. We'll laugh about how I almost believed she was a spirit.

"Frej-ja," one of the twins calls, as soon as I step through the door. They both come running with wooden blocks in their hands. I stay by the front door, clutching the door handle.

"Billy, Eddie, come here." Clementine catches them before they reach me. "You can play with Freja after your nap."

I'm scoffing the sandwich Maya has prepared for me, when Clementine comes downstairs again. She tells me that Mrs Lim's grandson might be coming over in the afternoon.

"Perhaps you and Jason can play a board game first, and then Maya can arrange a lovely little tea party for the four of you."

"Can't I go to his house?" I ask. That's bound to be better than Clementine's idea of a play date, and then I can just pop by on my way to the graveyard. She won't know how long I stay there.

While I'm listening, Clementine calls Mrs Lim to change the arrangement, telling her how good it will be for me to get out of the house.

But when I leave, a thunderstorm is brewing, so I give up on sneaking off to Bukit Brown. The large umbrella Clementine has lent me keeps my upper body dry. In Denmark, it's always windy, so horizontal drizzles hit you even if your umbrella doesn't pop inside-out. Here, the rain falls with the force of a shower.

The drops bounce off the ground up onto my bare legs. Water runs down the street, soaking my trainers. In the trench-like drain next to the pavement, a river carries dead leaves and bits of offerings.

"You should call her 'auntie'. *Ah Ma*, I mean," Jason says, as he leads me into the house, which is filled with gleaming dark furniture. Red fabric hangings with golden Chinese letters and shiny golden fringes decorate the walls. "It's a sign of respect towards elders here. You call them 'uncle' or 'auntie'."

"Oh, okay," I say, realizing that the woman from Dad's office wasn't related to the taxi driver.

"I'm telling you, because I know you don't know anything."

"I might not know anything about *ghosts*," I say.

A telly in the corner blares out incomprehensible shouts and background laughter.

"Since you know ab-so-lute-ly everything," I say, without hiding the sarcasm. "Can you tell me about those vampire ghosts?"

"*Pontianaks*? Why d'you wanna hear about them? They're the scariest, most horrible..." Jason pulls his shoulders up to his ears and shudders theatrically. "They have knife-sharp nails that they use to slice up a man's stomach before they eat his organs."

"Eek! Why would they do that?"

"Revenge! They're supposed to have died while they were pregnant or giving birth or something like that."

"So, you don't know?" I say it to tease him, but Jason pushes his long fringe to the side and glares at me.

We stand across from each other behind the couch. At howling laughter from the telly, Jason turns to face the screen. After a long pause where I'm trying to read the English subtitles, I say, "You can watch your show, if you want."

Just then, Mrs Lim comes out of the kitchen, wiping her hands on a tea towel. Today, she doesn't look the least bit scary.

"Wah!" she says, clapping a hand over her mouth, when she sees me. "How come she so tall?" she asks Jason, as if I can't understand her, and as if I'm a giant, though I'm only half a head taller than him.

We both shrug.

63

"Off the TV, boy." She picks up the tea towel and tells us to come and eat, mumbling about me being too thin.

"Maybe she eat already," Jason calls after her. "I don't think you'll like the food," he says to me.

"Why? Is it spicy?"

"Nah." His cheeks colour.

"Is it something exotic like tarantulas or crickets?" I ask. "That'd be brilliant."

Jason rolls his eyes. "No, that's what you get in Cambodia or Laos." He lowers his voice to a mutter. "It's frog porridge."

"Frog? I've always wanted to taste frog. D'you think I can help her prepare them?"

"She's already done that," he says with a sigh and opens the door to the kitchen.

While Mrs Lim sets the table, Jason says, "*Ah Ma*, Freja was running after a girl up to Bukit Brown the other day."

"Hmm..." She places one bowl with frog pieces and spring onion in a thick, dark-brown sauce and another with white porridge on the table, before she sits down.

I'm struggling to lift a sticky piece of frog with the chopsticks, until Jason picks one up with his fingers. At least there's a spoon for the porridge.

We eat in silence for a while. The frog legs are delicious and taste almost like chicken drumsticks. I'm wondering if I might sneak a couple of the bones into my pocket. Perhaps I can sharpen them with my knife and make them into needles or something.

"What this girl look like?" Mrs Lim asks.

"I think she's Chinese. Long black hair. And she's quite tall, actually, and thin."

"Thin girl with long, long neck?"

"Yes, auntie." Ling's neck is absurdly long.

"A child, is it?"

I nod, licking sauce off my fingers.

"*Aiyoh!* This one a very hungry ghost. Must remember ancestors and better make offerings." Mrs Lim shakes her head slowly. "Child spirit more difficult than adult one, because it never have time to enjoy life before dying."

"I don't understand... We don't have any ancestors here in Singapore. If she really is a ghost, then she must be someone else's hungry ghost."

"Mmm... Can be wandering ghost, but I never see this girl before."

"When I was following her, she led me to a gravestone..." I want to tell them about the Morse message, but my voice falters at Mrs Lim's shocked expression.

She raises one crooked, shaking forefinger, waving it at me. "*Cannot! Don't anyhow* follow ghosts."

I shudder. Sitting here, listening to Jason's *ah ma* talk about hungry ghosts as if they're real, it's difficult to doubt they exist. I have a creepy feeling that spirits surround me, wanting to be remembered. Suddenly, I don't want to hear another word about ghosts.

"Is that an eye?" I ask, pointing at a pearl-like glob in my bowl.

"Yeah, sorry. I hate those," Jason mumbles.

I pick the pearl up with thumb and forefinger and bring the small eyeball up for close inspection. "Can I eat it?"

"Ugh, gross."

Mrs Lim chuckles and tells me eating frog eyes is supposed

to strengthen your bones and improve your eyesight. When Jason looks away, I pop the eyeball into my mouth and swallow.

"Come. I show you offering," she says after we've eaten.

The rain has stopped. Outside, by the gate, Mrs Lim lights joss sticks, and hands me and Jason each a stack of paper money with colourful birds on one side. On the other side is a grey sketch of a temple. Above the amount is printed: *Hell Bank Note*. Before we light them, she explains that the smoke from burnt banknotes and other paper effigies is nectar for the spirits. It will feed them, so they are comfortable until next year.

"Isn't it a bit... morbid to spend so much time and energy on dead people?"

Mrs Lim takes my hand in both of hers. "Loss and grief is part of life," she says quietly. "We cannot forget the dead."

14

In the evening, after the twins are asleep, I'm sitting in the lounge, waiting for Dad to finish a phone call. Maya is tidying, putting wooden toys into a wicker basket. Clementine asks her to move a big vase with red exotic flowers.

"Didn't I tell you we can't have red colour in the north-west corner?" she says, "It's bad *chi*."

"Yes, ma'am." Maya moves the vase to the opposite corner of the room, by the kitchen door. "Is this good for *feng shui*, ma'am?"

"Yes, that's better. Anything red in this corner of the house might result in memory loss." Clementine flops down on one of the white sofas and starts telling me about *feng shui* and energy flows and the balance between *yin* and *yang*.

"It's so interesting," she says, "my *feng shui* consultant told me how Singapore's city planning is done to optimize the flow of *chi*, of energy."

I'm trying to hear if Dad has stopped talking on the phone, while Clementine drones on.

"*Feng shui* symbols are everywhere. Dragons in the east at the mouth of the river. The sports hub is in the shape of the black tortoise. The white tiger symbolized by Kent Ridge in the west. The vermillion bird of the south... Oh, I've forgotten what she said about the vermillion bird."

Dad's still on the phone, so I yawn and say I'm tired.

"Before you go... Your daddy told me you'd been up at Bukit Brown Cemetery."

"Mmm hmm..."

"The thing is, Freja, it's not a safe place to play. One of my friends saw a spitting cobra up there, and the ground is bound to be unstable, with all those hidden graves, and this time of year... So, you shouldn't run wild up there on your own."

"It's just nature," I say, while getting up. I'll talk to Dad about it in the morning—she can't decide what I do and where I go.

In my room, I sit by the open window. The cloudy sky is a muddy orange tonight. It's impossible to find even one bright star. I miss Mum. Last summer in Sweden, I didn't talk to her the whole week. Now, it's not yet been five days, but it feels longer. I also miss Dad. He's working so much, it's like he isn't here.

Before I go to bed, I scan the garden, but I can't see Ling.

On my phone, I read about hungry ghosts. Right now, according to the Chinese calendar, the gates to the realm of the dead are open, and the ghosts are on holiday in the real world. The streets are swarming with spirits, so it's a bit strange that Ling is the only one I've seen. But perhaps I've attracted her by breaking one of the many taboos. Going

68

swimming, wearing red and stepping in offerings are on the list of things to avoid during the seventh month. Nowhere does it say what you should do if a ghost needs your help.

When I'm almost dozing off, I wake with a jolt. In the silence, the stairs creak. I'm by the window, in an instant. Ling's standing under the palm tree, at the back of the lawn. Dad's walking towards her. Tonight, I don't waste time opening the window but run downstairs and outside.

When she sees me, Ling moves swiftly around Dad towards the gate to the street. Without noticing her, Dad continues on his path away from the house. By the parked car, she turns and waves for me to follow.

Damp grass tickles my toes, as I walk around the pool.

"Ling," I whisper, when I'm next to the car.

She's waiting outside the gate. She must've slid right through the bars. I think she's smiling. Her neck's even longer than I remembered. On her head, like a crown, is the garland of creepers I left on the gravestone. I recognize my sloppy splice of the ends. The plants should've been soaked by the rain. Instead, they seem fresher than when I made the yellow daisy chain.

That little detail—in combination with everything I've seen and heard and read—finally removes the last shred of doubt. There is no other explanation. Ling must be a ghost. A hungry ghost.

"I can't come with you now," I say. It's not that I'm scared, no matter what Jason's *ah ma* said, but I don't have any survival equipment on me, and I'm not even wearing flip-flops.

Ling's smile vanishes and a tear rolls down her cheek.

"Don't cry."

I glance back over my shoulder. Dad's right by the pool, walking towards us. He's looking straight at me, but it's as if he doesn't see me.

"I'll come to the graveyard tomorrow," I whisper. "I promise, I'll help you."

She turns and ducks out of sight behind the hedge.

Dad stops next to me, staring at the spot where Ling stood a moment ago. Then he turns round, his eyes passing over me, and walks back into the garden.

"Dad," I call. When he doesn't react, I run in front of him.

But it's like I'm behind a mirrored window. It happened once in the airport—I was waving at him and calling his name, but it was as if I was invisible. Only, this is worse, because there's no glass and he still can't see me. It's as if I don't exist. As if I'm not real.

"Dad." I tug at his arm. And then, like he's waking up, he blinks a couple of times and takes in the night-dark garden. He frowns at his watch.

It's almost one o'clock.

"I must've been sleepwalking." He rubs his eyes. "What a peculiar dream..."

"Did you see Ling?"

"Who?"

"The girl I told you about. She was here a moment ago."

"Please, Freja... Not again."

While we're walking back into the house, I keep glancing at Dad. The fruity scent from the trees with white-yellow artificial-looking flowers is strong. Frangipani, Clementine called them. It sounds like an Italian dessert, and right now they smell like overripe peaches.

70

I don't know what to say. Was he really sleepwalking?

At the top of the stairs, Dad gives me a half-hug. Before I slip back into my room, he whispers, "Best not say anything about this to Clementine. I don't want her to worry."

I lie awake afterwards, wondering what he doesn't want Clementine to worry about: his sleepwalking or the fact that their garden is haunted by a ghost.

After closing my eyes, I remember the uncanny sensation I had of ghosts surrounding me, when Jason's *ah ma* told me not to forget the dead. She said child spirits were more difficult because they hadn't had time to enjoy life. It makes me even more determined to help Ling.

15

On Saturday morning, Clementine wakes me at eight.

"You need to get over your jet lag before school on Monday," she says from the open door, holding the twins back. "*Fa-mi-ly time*," she sings, like a cheerleader in an American film.

Downstairs, I ask if we can go on the TreeTop Walk. I've seen photos of the suspension bridge between the treetops on the internet. In one of them, a row of monkeys is sitting on the handrail. The hike to the bridge is along a trail through a nature reserve. But Clementine says the trail's too bumpy and the boardwalk has too many stairs for the twin's pushchair.

"How about a trip to the zoo?" she asks. "You three little monkeys can meet some real monkeys. Wouldn't that be fun, Freja?"

I nod and try to ignore that she treats me as if I'm five years old.

The visit to the zoo is kind of nice. After we have breakfast with the orangutangs—literally sitting down with them on the terrace railing by our table—I see white tigers for the first time. Their eyes are the palest blue, like the sea in Denmark on a winter morning. Dad goes with me into the reptile zone, where I hold a live python, while Clementine and the twins stay outside. All morning, he hardly looks at his phone.

In the afternoon, Dad heads to his office in the city. He has to pick up a folder. On a Saturday! But I'm glad, because even though I want to show him the graveyard, today I'd rather go alone, so I can find Ling or at least see if she's answered my question.

I tell Clementine I'm going to prepare for school and relax in my bedroom.

"Don't fall asleep and don't forget we're going out tonight," she calls after me, with her gaze fixed on the stream of updates on her screen.

Standing on the ledge outside my window, I throw my green climbing rope over a wooden roof beam above. Then I balance on my toes and tie a bowline knot.

From her perch on the inside of the glass, Lizzie blinks at me. Her little head veers from side to side, as if she doesn't understand why I can't run down the wall like a lizard.

After tying double overhand stopper knots at regular intervals, I wind the rope up and let it hang, shielded by the tree's leaves. I hope no one sees it and thinks it's a green viper.

The mud-splattered combat trousers I left on my bathroom floor after my last trip to Bukit Brown have been washed and folded and even ironed. I make a mental note to thank Maya and tell her she shouldn't waste her time ironing my clothes. Within minutes they'll be wrinkled, anyway.

73

Before I unfurl the rope and climb out the window, I fill my pockets with my survival equipment and two granola bars. On the ground, I tie the rope to a branch, so it's hidden. On Thursday, I stashed the stick, the root-rope and my muddy hiking boots in the tree. The hiking boots are wedged in between low branches close to the trunk, and they're sole-up so they won't get wet inside if it rains. It's a trick Dad taught me in Sweden. "Just check for snakes", he usually teased, although the common viper is the only venomous snake in Scandinavia, and the weather was too cold for them. Here in Singapore, many snakes are venomous, so I shake the boots well before I put them on.

I slip out of the gate and backtrack to the sign I made on the trail next to the expressway. Despite the rain yesterday, it's still there: five crumbled bricks stacked on top of a banana-palm leaf. This was where I emerged from the wilderness. All other signs of my last expedition have already been erased by the rainforest.

With my phone in one hand, I stomp north, banging the stick into the ground, watching the blue dot on my screen get closer and closer to the yellow star I used to mark the gravestone.

The nearer I get, the more anxious I become. What if Ling isn't in the little grove? What if she hasn't left a message, answering my *Who are you* question? What if she's left one before it rained, and it's washed away? What if CQD was just a random scatter of pebbles and sticks? Perhaps she never left me a message.

I try to prepare myself for disappointment.

But I'm not disappointed. A long line of pebbles and sticks

lies on the flat stone. With one glance, it's clear that it isn't the pattern I made.

../-.. ---/-. --- -/
.-. . -- . -- -... . .-.

"Ling!" I call, although I already sense that she isn't here. Sweltering heat, and noise from the cicada orchestra, close in on me. I don't need to write anything down to read what it says, but I photograph and copy the Morse code into my notebook. She's written:

I DO NOT REMEMBER

I wonder if that's why she has latched on to me, because she can't remember who her family is. Or were.

Not being able to remember must be awful. Perhaps she used to live in Dad's house more than a hundred years ago, when 'CQD' was still in use. Perhaps that's why she keeps coming back to the garden.

While I'm speculating, I collect pebbles and sticks, because I need more than the bits she's used for my message.

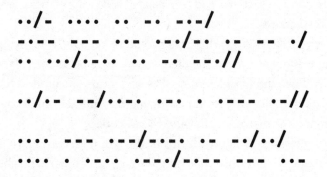

../- .... .. -- -../
-.-- --- ... .-./-. .. -- ./
.. .../.-.. .. -- ---//

../.- --/.... ... . .--- .-//

.... --- .-./-.. .. --/../
.... . .-.. .--./-.-- --- ...

I THINK YOUR NAME IS LING

I AM FREJA

HOW CAN I HELP YOU

It begins to rain, pouring from the first drops. I unwrap the granola bars and place them inside the wilted garland of creepers.

Within minutes my T-shirt's soaked, but I'm not at all cold. Instead of heading back towards the expressway, I walk uphill in the other direction. When I catch a glimpse of white through the trees, I run after it, believing it's Ling. But it's just two blonde women in white summer dresses. They're strolling along one of the asphalt pathways, under tiny umbrellas.

Hidden by a cluster of banana trees, I watch them. Their dresses cling to their legs, and, with every step they take, water sprays out of their sandals. Despite that and the torrential rain, they're chatting and laughing and pausing to read a small sign next to the path.

After they're gone, I study the sign. *The Paupers' Section, 1922–73*, it says at the top. Below, a text explains that the poor, or people without families, were buried in this low-lying area, which has bad *feng shui* because water flows there and stagnates.

1922. That's the earliest Ling could've been buried here. If she was my age when she died, she must've been born after 1910. The *Titanic* sank in 1912—I looked it up—and used CQD. It could fit. But why would a pauper girl from that time know a maritime distress signal and Morse code?

I'm trying to figure all this out, when it strikes me that perhaps it's not only that Ling doesn't remember who she was or her family. Perhaps it's worse. Perhaps she didn't even have a family and died all alone.

Sadness stabs inside my stomach. Because what could be worse than dying and no one remembering that you ever existed?

16

Instead of following the path out of the cemetery, I make my way back to Ling's grave. I want her to know that I won't abandon her. When I saw her in the garden last night, she was so very sad. Perhaps she thought I'd break my promise to help her. Perhaps she thought I'd forget about her, too.

The moment I stand up after squeezing through the bushes around the little grove, I glance over at the flat grave-stone. My long message has already been replaced by a much shorter one.

-..-. --- -- ./.-- .. - ..../ -- .

Rushing to get closer, I slip on the swampy ground. While I get up and wipe my muddy hands on my trousers, I decode the pattern:

COME WITH ME

I'm about to take a picture of the message, when a tingle down my spine makes me look up. Ling stands by the edge of the grove, waving me towards her. It only takes a flip of my hand to turn the lens in her direction, but, before I can snap a photo, she's disappeared between the shrubs.

"Wait," I call, slipping my phone back in the side pocket of my combats. Without caring about the scratching thorns, I crash through the bushes.

Outside the grove, I chase after her. Like the time she led me to the gravestone, Ling waits for me whenever I can't keep up. While I'm running, I wonder where she'll lead me. Perhaps she has a treasure trove somewhere in the graveyard, filled with keepsakes that'll give me clues to who she was.

From the low-lying paupers' section, we run uphill past impressive graves with decorated tiles and statues of turban-wearing, armed guards. The ground in front of some of them is littered with mushed burnt paper and soggy food offerings.

An old man shuffles along an asphalt pathway in too-big plastic sandals, too-short trousers and a faded football shirt. Just before I reach him, he starts yelling in Chinese.

He grabs the sleeve of my T-shirt and switches to English, shouting, "Stop, girl!" Scattered, yellow teeth stick out of his gaping mouth in odd directions. His head turns to look after Ling, as if he can actually see her, then back at me.

Further uphill, Ling stops.

"*Cannot* follow this one ghost," he says. "Bad. Bad, bad!"

"Why?" Jason's *ah ma* said the exact same thing yesterday. But her talk of ghosts creeped me out. Now I wish I'd asked her what she meant. "Why can't I follow her?"

He repeats, "Bad, bad," and speaks on urgently in a mix of Singlish and Chinese that I wish I could understand, while shaking his head.

When I glance back uphill, Ling's gone. I pull away, mumbling, "Sorry." The seam of my T-shirt tears. I'm not scared of Ling, and I promised her I'd help.

With the man yelling after me, I race up to where she stood and continue through a tunnel of elephant ear-like leaves. On the other side, the rainforest becomes less dense.

I emerge on a grassy hill. At its top, an enormous banyan tree rises from the ground. Its branches, with their curtains of hanging roots, spread out above me, like a gigantic parasol with floor-length fringes. Close to the trunk, the aerial roots have matured into slender trunks themselves and surround the tree like prison bars. In an opening between them, I catch sight of Ling's white dress and long black hair.

I slow to a walk and circle the tree, searching for an entrance between the stiffened roots. On the inside, Ling's matching my pace, walking around the trunk of the host tree, so that she is framed by roots when we reach an opening at the same time.

"Hi Ling," I say.

"Frej-y-a?" she whispers tentatively.

"Freja, rhymes with Maya." I smile to show her she pronounced it almost right, then ask, "Do you speak English?"

She nods and reaches for my hand. All I feel is a wave of cool air, like when you stick your hand in the freezer to take an ice lolly. A shiver runs up my arm.

Turned sideways, I edge myself gingerly through the narrow gap and behind the wall of roots. The ground in the hushed space is dry, despite the rain. Above, the branches of the tree are so high up, I can't even touch them with my arms stretched out. Together, we walk around the massive trunk, inside the cage of banyan tree roots. Brown leaves crackle under my feet. Stripes of weak light fall through the bars. It's the most magical hiding place I've ever seen. I wish I could live in a den just like this—perhaps weave grass between the roots to shield against the wind—and stay in the wilderness.

When we're back at the opening, I turn towards Ling. Even though my clothes are soaked and dirty, her white dress is clean and dry. She's as tall as me, but skeletally thin. On her neck, every sinew and every bone are visible, and it's twice as long as my rather long neck; that wasn't a trick of light.

"I want to help you," I say. "If you tell me what you remember, then I'm sure we can figure out who you were... Are, I mean." Does she even realize she's dead?

"I... I do not remember anything." Her voice is hoarse, like she hasn't used it in a long time. "I do not even know when I died."

I exhale with relief, glad I won't have to explain that she's a ghost. "Why did you come to our garden?"

She shakes her head. "It felt like coming home."

"So you think you used to live there?"

"No. I..." She hesitates. "Last time, and all the times before, when they let us out, I never knew where to go... But this time, I did. I saw him. The man with yellow hair—"

"My dad?"

She nods. "And you. Your eyes... their blue colour... they remind me of someone... Someone from long before I was forgotten. I thought you would remember me. More than anything, I wish to be remembered."

"But I don't know who you are," I say, then see the tears gathering in her dark eyes. "Not yet. I'll help you find out. I promise. I'll start by asking you loads of questions to jog your memory, okay?"

I try to take her hand, but my fingers pass through hers, until they're making a fist.

"D'you know when you were born? And how old you were when you died?"

She shakes her head.

I can't even tell if she's younger or older than me.

"Open your mouth wide, like this." I gape. "And say, 'Ahhh'."

When she copies me, I count her teeth. She has fourteen lower teeth, but only thirteen upper teeth. I smile, thinking it's handy to have a dentist mum, before I remember that Mum isn't a dentist at the moment. She's the one being treated for something far worse than a toothache.

"You don't have all your twelve-year molars yet, so you must've been around twelve years old. Like me. Could that be right?"

She shrugs.

"How come you know Morse code? Were you a scout?"

"What is a scout?"

"It's... That doesn't matter. 'CQD' hasn't been used in about one hundred years. D'you also know 'SOS'?" I ask, hoping she doesn't.

Instead, she nods.

I sigh. The *Titanic* could've sunk in Ling's lifetime if she were among the first people buried here. But she could just as well have lived much later, if someone like Clementine's father taught her both distress signals.

I'm not sure what else to ask her, and I'm starting to realize how difficult it will be to find out who she was, if she doesn't remember anything at all. Perhaps we have to do this differently. Take things a bit slower. If I get to know her better, perhaps something she says or does will give me clues.

—17—

"Why don't we play a game?" I suggest, although I should be getting back before Clementine discovers I'm gone. It's almost five o'clock. "Let's pretend that we've travelled back in time to when you were alive. Without thinking too much about it, you show me the way to where you used to live. Okay?"

Ling nods. But when we emerge from the tree, she begins to cry, saying, "I don't know where to go."

"Don't cry. That never helps..."

It's still raining, so we go back into the den under the banyan tree. I'm trying to find a way to trigger her memory. Ling has stopped crying.

"Let's say... Let's say we're still in your time. What would you be doing on a Saturday afternoon?"

"Doing?"

"I mean, would you read or play or work or..." What did girls do a hundred years ago? "Perhaps sew, or write letters?"

Ling shrugs and shakes her head.

But I'm not giving up. "Did you like to play outside? With a ball? Or hide-and-seek or tag or hopscotch?"

"I liked chasing someone in the garden," Ling says with a big smile.

"Good. Tag, it is." I set off at a run around the massive trunk, yelling, "Catch me!" She's so fast I need every advantage I can get.

Although I can't hear her, I know she's gaining on me. I've passed the narrow opening to the outside for the third time, when I feel a breath of cool air on my neck and she cries, "Tag!"

Ling pirouettes and floats in the other direction. I scramble to follow, chasing after her. The roots and the stripes of light blur together. After three rounds, she's so far ahead, she's on the opposite side of the trunk. Hoping that I can tag her when she catches up, I stop abruptly. But the circle of stiffened roots continues to rotate. With a hand on the tree, I try to steady myself. A moment later, Ling is next to me, but I'm too light-headed to tag her.

The root cage turns faster. It's spinning round and round like on the meteorite fair-ground ride I tried once with my cousins. To avoid being pushed outward, I hold on to a gnarl on the trunk. Brown leaves whirl around me. What's happening?

The light dims. Flickering in and out of sight, overlaying the trunk, towering double doors, with golden handles, appear in the gloom. The sight of them fills me with dread. I tear my hand away from the trunk, as if I've been burnt.

Immediately, the centrifugal force throws me against the bars of the cage. Ling lands next to me with a yelp. She's asking me why she can feel pain, but I'm winded and trying to listen to the sounds from behind the towering doors. There are whispers. Sighs. A small child crying.

I never ever want to see what's behind those doors. But who's crying? I have to find out. Pushing off from the root bars, I fling myself through the whirlwind, towards the trunk. As I touch one of the golden handles, the doors begin to open.

Behind me, Ling yells, "No!"

Dark-grey light, the colour of thunderclouds, spills out of the crack. The child cries again. The sound cuts through me, piercing my heart.

Ling yanks my arm back, and we both slam against the roots. The sounds mute. The doors disappear. We're still spinning.

After a while, the darkness fades and the turning slows. Glimmers of light from outside change from dots to dashes, until we stop. The flurry of dead leaves settles on the ground. Then all is still.

"What just happened?" I whisper. Whatever it was felt too real to be pretend. I could never have imagined those towering doors or that heart-wrenching cry.

Ling takes my hand. I feel a jolt at her cool, firm touch. There's nothing ghostlike about her grip now.

"Freja, you are not supposed to enter the realm of the dead, while you are still alive."

"Was that... behind the doors... ?" I ask, shuddering.

"Yes," she says, and leads me through the opening between the roots.

Outside, it isn't raining any more. The sunlight's so bright it makes me blink. Then I blink again and rub my eyes, because the cemetery's gone.

We're still on a peak under the branches of the enormous banyan tree. Around us, everything's green, like before, but the hill seems to somehow have grown higher. Apart from the banyan tree, there's only sparse vegetation up here, so we have a clear view of the landscape. Below, mist rises from a rainforest that stretches all the way to the ocean.

It's as if we've travelled to a different world beyond my wildest dreams.

"Where are we?" I ask.

"Singapore?" Ling says hesitantly.

In the distance, green bumps pop out of the empty sea. They resemble the small islands I saw from Dad's office. But if this is Singapore, then where are the container ships? The buildings? The people?

"When? Are we in your time? Can you find the way to your house?" But even as I'm asking, I realize Singapore couldn't have been this uninhabited wilderness a hundred years ago.

"I think..." Ling gazes at me with her dark eyes. "I think, we are at the beginning. When the universe was in balance."

I take it all in again. The beginning of what? 'In balance'? If she means undisturbed by humans, then we've come to the right place. It's so very peaceful. I can't even hear the noisy birds or cicadas. Except for the rising mist, there's no movement anywhere.

I've hardly finished the thought, when I see glints of brightness out in the ocean. Could it be a Morse code signal from a heliograph? I squint, trying to decode the sequence. But there are no breaks between the blinking dots, and they're not all coming from the exact same spot. Something shiny's floating in the sea, but it isn't someone holding a mirror and trying to send a message by reflecting the sunlight. Before I can point it out to Ling, the brightness vanishes below the surface.

"I don't understand how we got here, Ling."

"This banyan tree is magical," she says. "I have heard other spirits call it the wishing tree. I always hide in there and wish to remember. To be remembered. Nothing like this has ever happened before."

"Then why aren't we where you lived? Why would the tree send us to this wild—" Suddenly, I remember wishing that I could stay and live in the tree den for ever. Is this my wish coming true? Have I accidentally taken us here? And how will we get back to the real world?

What's Dad going to do if I never return? Or Mum?

Calm down, Freja, I try to tell myself. But no matter how many deep breaths I take, they don't help. I'm prepared for wilderness, but not for this... this...

"Perhaps we can find my memories somewhere." Ling wanders out of the banyan tree's shade.

I stay rooted to the ground. *Think, Freja! What are you supposed to do if you get lost in the wilderness? Find landmarks to orient yourself.*

While scanning the horizon for anything familiar, I reach into both side pockets. My trousers are dry. I pull my phone out first, but it's dead. From the other pocket, I extract my compass and the map. It has gone white along the folds, as if it's been through both a washing machine and a tumbler. The needle on my compass spins like the long arm of a clock in a time-lapse video, before it stops.

I'm facing south-east, in the direction where the city centre with the skyscrapers and weird buildings would be, if this was Singapore. But all I see are treetops, bordered by the vast ocean.

Practical tasks calm me down, so I try to compare the coastline with the map. There's an island straight south that could be Sentosa.

"Freja, nooo!" Ling screams from somewhere on the other side of the tree.

I run to her and gasp at the sight that meets me.

Beyond our grassy hill, and for as far as I can see, red, high-rise flames shoot up into billowing, black smoke. The rainforest is burning.

"Not in balance," Ling says.

For a while, we stand in silence, watching the forest-eating wildfire. The sight's mesmerizing. The blaze is north-west of where we're standing. Red in the north-west. I remember Clementine saying something about that. What was it again? Something her *feng shui* guru had told her. Something about the lounge being all white because it was in the north-western corner of the house.

Something about red in that corner causing memory loss.

—18—

A large bird rises out of the flames. From here, its wings appear to be on fire. I squint, trying to recognize the bird, and wish I'd brought binoculars. Its wingbeats are slow, like those of a bird of prey. If we've somehow gone far back in time, perhaps it a Pterosaur.

The bird swoops down into the sea of flames again.

"Oh! We have to help it," I say, although it's too far away for us to do anything.

Moments later, the bird reappears out of the smoke much closer to us. It flies over the banyan tree, leaving a charcoal trail in the sky. When it's right above us, its long narrow beak opens and it lets out a burst of orange light and a cry that sounds almost human.

Something falls out of the sky, swirling round and round like a helicopter seed from a maple tree, and lands at our feet. A red feather. Its tip is scorched.

"Was that a phoenix?" I ask, picking up the feather and twirling it between my fingers. The bird didn't look like the phoenixes I've seen in films and books. An unpleasant burnt smell, like the time I singed my hair on the campfire because I'd forgotten to tie it back, comes off the feather. It's so long that the blackened tip sticks out, after I've put it in my biggest pocket.

"My mother called it the vermillion bird."

"The vermillion bird of the south?" I ask. Clementine mentioned that too. "Oh, you remember your mother?"

"I have this glimpse of waking up next to her..." Ling closes her eyes. "Ma is asleep on our mat. Her hair is out of its usual tight bun. Long strands tickle my toes. Light creeps under the door into our windowless room. I hear sounds from the nursery and open the door a crack, to see who is there, whether it is safe to come out."

"What do you mean 'safe'?"

"I... I do not remember."

Nearby, a high-pitched wail pierces the air. It must be the vermillion bird, but it sounds like a baby. It's as if I'm in Ling's memory, hearing a baby cry from the room next door. As if I'm the one who's remembering.

A smoky breeze makes me cough.

North of us, a sprawling lake that resembles a lizard with too many legs, is blocking the wildfire. But, to the west, the blaze advances. At the bottom of the hill, flames lick at the trees.

Roaring, a bulky white shape shoots out of the inferno. It bounds up the slope, in our direction.

"The white tiger of the west," Ling says.

"Shouldn't we run?" How can she stand there so calmly? A tiger is running straight at us.

91

But perhaps nothing can harm us here. Perhaps this place isn't even real? I don't think I'm dreaming, but I pinch my forearm. It smarts.

The tiger's twice as big as the white tiger I saw at the zoo. It gets so close to us I see the panic in its pale-blue eyes. Then it leaps towards us—and vanishes below the ground.

An ear-splitting roar reverberates over the hill.

Ling pulls me forward, one careful step at a time, until we stand at the edge of a large pit in the ground. Inside, the white tiger springs up and throws itself against the walls, growling. But the pit is deep and its sides almost vertical. The tiger can't escape.

Dried grass is scattered across the ground beneath it. One of its hind legs is stuck in a net of lianas. The tiger thrashes to get free. Instead, it gets more entangled with every jump. Someone must've covered the pit with a net of lianas woven with grass, camouflaging the huge hole in the ground. There's no doubt the pit is meant to be a trap.

I survey the hill, expecting to see a flock of hunters emerging from a hidden camp.

"Ling, it's too dangerous to stay here with that forest fire... and whoever has built this trap might be coming soon. We should leave. If we can."

"Yes," Ling says. "Something is wrong here."

At the sound of our voices, the white tiger stops struggling. It looks up, its blue eyes pleading, and I wish we could set it free.

When we walk back up to the tree, the deep growls begin again.

"How are we going to get back?"

Ling shakes her head.

"Let me think... It was as if the spinning transported us here. You said you've often been inside the tree, making wishes. Did you always sit still?"

"Yes."

"Okay. We were running, so perhaps that's what we need to do to get the tree to spin."

We've reached the opening in the roots, and I cast a last glance out over the rainforest and the ocean. The eastern side of the island is still peaceful. I hope it will stay that way, and that something stops the wildfire before it destroys this magical place.

Inside the ring of roots, I ask, "Which way?"

"We ran one way first and then the other," Ling says.

"You're right." I pause to remember. "We ran clockwise— three rounds—then anticlockwise."

I take Ling's hand and give it a squeeze before we start running.

"Think about my father," I shout, when we turn. To be absolutely sure I'm returning to the right place, I think about Clementine and the twins too.

"My father," Ling repeats.

I want to correct her, tell her she shouldn't think about her father, but her hand slips from mine. We're in the wind tunnel. Dead leaves spiral around us, and everything's spinning. My body presses against the root cage. I close my eyes to avoid seeing the towering gates. Too late to stop me from hearing the wails, I cover my ears with my hands.

When the surroundings stop revolving, I'm lying curled up under a brown cover of leaves.

"Did it work?" I ask, getting up.

No one answers. It's almost dark inside the tree.

"Ling!" I walk around the trunk, but she isn't here.

Outside, it's raining. I stumble out of the opening, as a crack of thunder booms above. Gravestones jut out of the undergrowth around me. Hanging roots from the banyan tree's long branches are tangled into other trees further down the hill. I'm back in the real world.

"Ling!" I call again. Where is she?

If she thought about her own father, perhaps the wishing tree took her to the time when she was alive. Perhaps that will make her remember. Or she might've ended up in the realm of the dead, if that's where her father is. I shudder and cross my fingers, hoping she's safe.

A flash lights up the banyan tree, followed by another boom, and I start jogging. It's too dangerous to be in a forest in this weather. Within minutes, my clothes are soaked again.

When I reach the cemetery gate, I slow to a walk. My phone pings. I tear it out of my pocket. The ping's a reminder about our dinner plans in one hour.

My phone's working normally again. For a moment, I wonder if it was all really just make-believe. But as I push my phone back into the pocket, something tickles my hand. It's the singed tip of the long, red feather.

—19—

While I'm winding the rope up, after climbing in through my window, there's a knock on my door. Has anyone seen me get back? I run into the en-suite bathroom, as the door to my room opens.

"Freja," Clementine calls. "Don't forget we're going out in half an hour."

"Taking a shower now!" I peel off my soaked clothes and hide them under a towel, in case she comes in here.

"It's a very nice restaurant... Could you wear a dress? Perhaps the white one I got you?"

Pretending I haven't heard her question, I turn on the shower, because there's no way I'm putting on a dress.

Perhaps if I tell Dad I'm not feeling well, he'll let me stay home. Then I can wait here for Ling. I'm worried about her. I desperately hope she'll come back tonight, so I know nothing bad has happened to her. That she's safe.

I wonder what it means, that she remembered checking to see if it was safe to leave her bedroom. Why wouldn't it have been safe?

Showers are good for mulling things over. Sometimes too good—too many thoughts flood my mind at once. Glimpses of the things we saw in that other world with the mythical creatures come rushing in. The white tiger of the west and the phoenix-like vermillion bird. The curious blinking brightness in the empty sea, east of the island. And the raging wildfire.

Could Ling's memory loss really be linked to the red flames in the north-west? Are Clementine's beliefs in the influence of energy flows true?

The spray of water pounds on my scalp and shoulders. It makes me think of rain. I wonder if that would be enough to extinguish the forest fire. Perhaps then, Ling could remember more. But there were no clouds in the blue sky, and what else could put out a wildfire?

After the shower, I cram my wet hair into a ponytail and put on a T-shirt—white even—and clean shorts with the bare necessities of survival equipment in their pockets.

In the twins' room, Maya has dressed both boys in white trousers. She's trying to button a striped light-blue shirt on one of them before he can wiggle away. Clementine's overseeing her from the doorway in a long blue dress. Her shiny hair falls in soft waves. She frowns when she sees what I'm wearing.

"We're leaving soon, Freja. It's okay to get dressed now," she says as if she doesn't know this is what I plan to wear. "Do you want me to do your hair?"

"What's wrong with my hair?"

"Nothing... It looks... nice. But we could blow-dry it and plait it into a crown. Or how about a French braid?"

"I like it like this."

When Dad comes out of their bedroom, buttoning his own light-blue shirt, she says, "Could you help me a moment, Will?"

The only word I catch before I go back into my room is "dress", so it's no surprise when Dad follows me.

"I don't like dresses." I stand by the window, peering into the garden, without turning.

"Please, Freja," he says. "It means a lot to Clementine. The restaurant is one of her main sponsors."

I don't understand why She needs sponsors. It's not like she's doing any sports. "Can't I stay at home, Dad?"

"I'd like for you to come, and so would Clementine." He places a hand on my shoulder.

"You know, Dad, the girl I saw in the garden last night, she's actually a ghost."

"Freja... Please..."

I swivel to face him, shaking off his hand. "She isn't imaginary. She's a hungry ghost, and she's somehow connected to us. That's why she haunts the garden! She remembers someone with blue eyes like ours. From like a hundred years ago. Did everyone in our family have blue eyes, d'you think?"

Dad shakes his head. His eyes are sad. "You really are too old for imaginary friends."

"I'm telling you, she's not imaginary. Her name's Ling, and she's—"

"Freja, please stop." Dad presses his fingers against his temples.

He seems so worried; I decide I won't talk to him about Ling again until I've discovered who she was when she was alive. "O-kay, I'll wear a dress," I say to make him smile.

Both dresses are too short and flimsy to hide combat shorts, but the dress with pink dots at least has pockets deep enough for my Swiss Army knife.

After dinner, the owner of the restaurant comes over to chat with us. Or, rather, with Her. Clementine talks and talks, even more than usual, about her fancy party. I don't listen and keep glancing at my watch. While Dad takes Eddie to the loo, Billy's eating olives. I'm watching him closely, afraid he might choke on a stone.

When we get home, I sit in my open window, twirling the red feather, hoping Ling will return. The rain has stopped. It's taken the smell of bonfires away. The air feels almost cool. Twice, I climb down and take a stroll around the garden, calling for Ling.

Why isn't she coming? What's happened to her?

At one o'clock, she still hasn't appeared.

—20—

The moment I wake up, I want to go to the cemetery and search for Ling. But I can't, because I can't climb out of my window or get hold of my hiking boots or even leave the house without anyone noticing. Billy and Eddie and Dad are in the garden. Through a gap in the curtains, I watch them play football. The twins are so funny and cute. When one of them stumbles and falls, he doesn't even cry, because Dad is right there and tickles him. In the end, Dad's the one lying down with both boys crawling all over him. They're so happy.

"We should wake up Freja," Clementine says, coming out from the house.

"Where Frej-ja?" one of the twins asks, then starts shouting my name.

"Shhh, Eddie, she's still sleeping," Dad says.

A couple of days ago, I thought they were completely identical, with their dark eyes and black shiny hair that stands up at the back, but there are small differences: a mole on Eddie's neck, a scar across Billy's forehead. And Eddie is chubbier. Billy is as thin as I was in baby photos. For a moment, I want to open the curtains and shout, "I'm here!" to see their reaction.

Dad extracts himself from the twins and throws the ball to the far end of the garden. Like puppies, they chase after it.

"Let her sleep a bit longer," he says, and sits down. His bare feet on the sun lounger stick out from under the covered terrace.

"It would be good for her to come outside and spend time with the boys. I don't understand why she doesn't want anything to do with them."

The twins have kicked the ball under the frangipani trees and are busy tearing flowers off the low branches. They're chatting and one of them keeps saying, "Frej-ja."

I'd hoped it would be much easier to avoid them, that they would ignore me if I ignored them. They don't.

Dad murmurs something I can't hear.

"Did you notice yesterday at the zoo, when Eddie took her hand and wanted to drag her over to the giraffe? She shook him off and turned away. He was so disappointed..."

"I'm worried about her. I think she has an imaginary friend again," Dad lowers his voice. "She had that when... after it happened... when Marianne was... coming here... perhaps it's too much... makes me sad..."

Although I'm standing stock-still, I can't hear all he's saying. This is precisely what I didn't want to happen. Now that I'm here, Dad's becoming sad. I've even made little Eddie unhappy.

"Let's hope it'll get better when she starts school," Clementine says. "Perhaps she just needs to get out and about, instead of moping in her room. Why don't we go to the beach?"

Maya's off on Sundays, so I gulp a glass of orange juice and eat a bowl of cereal, like I would've at home, before we get into the car. I'm sitting in the back, squeezed in between the two toddler car seats. We haven't even left the driveway when Eddie prods me with his board book.

To make up for yesterday's giraffe incident, I read *The Very Hungry Caterpillar* to him seven times. Billy keeps throwing his toy car down on the floor and whinges until I pick it up. Clementine's curled around her seat, turned backwards, shushing Billy and pleading with him to listen to the story. She interrupts my reading more times than him to tell me about buildings and places we pass.

Dad isn't on the phone, but I don't think he's listening to us. I keep glancing at him in the rear-view mirror to see if he looks sad.

After what feels like for ever, we drive across a causeway to an island. Its name, *Sentosa*, is written in elephant-sized letters on an arch that spans two fake medieval towers. Behind it, a small fairy-tale castle with countless turrets outshines two roller coasters.

"Were there ever lions here, Dad?" I ask, when we pass a colossal statue of a merlion with a viewing terrace in its mouth. There's a photo of a smaller merlion in the tourist guide Aunt Astrid bought me. *Singapura* means 'the lion city' and this unfamiliar half-fish, half-lion is the city's mascot.

"No. Only tigers, I believe," Clementine replies.

"White tigers? Like the one—" I stop myself before I can say, *Like the one I saw with Ling.* I can still remember the panic and pleading in its pale-blue eyes. "The one in the zoo?"

"Zoo! Zoo! Zoo!" Billy chants. "Want Zoo."

"No, Billy. Today, we're going to the beach," Clementine says, getting out of the car in the car park.

"The other day, you talked about the vermillion bird of the south and the white tiger of the west..."

"Yes?" Clementine stands up after strapping Eddie into the double stroller.

"I'll take the boys," Dad says. "You girls go ahead."

"I can't remember where you said the other animals could be found."

"The mythical creatures are metaphors linked to Chinese astrology. They aren't actually real, Freja." A row of waves appears on Clementine's forehead above her oversized sunglasses. "I'll ask my *feng shui* consultant to come round and explain the details, if you're interested."

I shrug. "But there's a dragon and a turtle, right?"

"Yes. The black tortoise of the north and the azure dragon of the east."

An image of the terrapins in the lake at the Botanic Gardens swims into my head. There was a lake north of the banyan tree. A lake full of water. Maybe that's where the black tortoise lives. It isn't an ordinary animal but a mythical creature. If we found it, perhaps it could help us put out the fire.

In my mind, I'm already sketching the beginning of a plan. But what's the point if Ling doesn't come back? Fear gnaws at me, growing a knot in my belly.

"We're here!" Clementine leads us to parasol-covered deckchairs in the fenced-in enclosure of a beach club. It's very organized, with proper menus and waiters. There's even a swimming pool for people who aren't keen on seawater and don't want to come into contact with the sand. I've never seen a pool on a beach before—it seems kind of unnecessary, like putting a T-shirt on over sunscreen. Which is exactly what Clementine does to Billy and Eddie. Both are lathered in a white creme under their rash guards.

I play ball with Dad and the boys for a little while, but as soon as Dad flops down on a lounger, I escape to the edge of the sea. Clementine keeps the twins in the baby pool. There's even a lifeguard, so I don't have to worry. Sitting alone on the fine, yellow sand with my legs in the green sea, I let the waves lap at my swimsuit, but I can't stop fretting about Ling. My insides tie themselves into granny knots.

The beach is sheltered behind small artificial islands with palm trees. Between them, I'm trying to spot something that resembles the curious floating brightness I saw from the banyan tree, but a wall of container ships blocks my view of the horizon.

Loud music blasts from speakers behind the pool, which is so full of people that they're standing in the chest-deep water. I glance back at Dad—I thought he would hate a place like this. It couldn't be more different from the peaceful wilderness of the Swedish lakes. He's lying on a lounger in the shade. He must've fallen asleep, because his phone has slid out of his hand and is sticking vertically out of the sand. Perhaps he was sleepwalking again last night. I wish I could ask him if he saw Ling.

Before driving home, we have tea at the beach club. I order a burger, but when it arrives, I can only eat a few bites. I press my fists against my navel.

"Oh dear," Clementine says. "It looks like you're getting one of those awful tummy aches. Are you nervous about school?"

I remove my hands and shake my head. To be honest, I haven't thought about school. What with worrying about Ling and Mum and making everyone sad... I'd almost forgotten I'm starting school tomorrow. Somehow my brain has kept it a secret.

—21—

Clementine drives me to school, although I tell her I'd be fine on the school bus. My hands are squeezed between my knees, to stop them from cradling my aching belly. I'm thinking about Ling. Last night, I stayed up till midnight, waiting, but she didn't turn up.

Outside the school gates, Clementine gets out of the car, while pushing her sunglasses up into her hair.

"You don't have to come. Dad showed me the reception on Friday," I say. I can't believe he isn't here. But when I got up this morning, he was on his way out the door, travelling to Manila or Malacca or Mumbai. Somewhere starting with M.

"I'm sure your mum would take you all the way." Clementine reaches over and adjusts the collar of my polo shirt. When I pull back, she lets her hand drop.

I almost answer that she isn't my mum. "She wouldn't," I say instead. "You don't know her."

Clementine looks away into the playground where kids are milling around. "I suppose I don't." She slides the sunglasses back into place. "Would you like me to pick you up after—"

"I'll take the school bus."

She stands there for a moment, and I realize she's about to give me a hug. But I don't want *her* to give me a hug on my first day in a new school. I want Dad. Or Mum.

"Bye." I slip through the gate before she can touch me.

"Good luck, Freja!" She calls so loudly several people turn in her direction. Slumping, I try to hide behind my school bag, while I hurry towards the reception. I expect a teacher will bring me to the classroom, where I can sit in a corner, feeling awkward and new. After such a catastrophic beginning to the day, I just want to get it over with, so I can return to the graveyard and search for Ling.

But I've only been waiting for five minutes, when two girls run into the reception area.

"Are you Freja?" one of them gasps, brushing a mass of red curls out of her freckled face.

"Yes."

"I'm Kiera. This is Sunitha." She tugs at the arm of the other girl, who beams at me with warmth in her dark eyes.

"We're your buddies," Sunitha says.

"We'll show you everything, and you can ask us absolutely anything about anything." Kiera flings her arms outwards.

"First, we'll take you up to registration in our class-room," explains Sunitha. "You have to be there at ten to eight every morning." She leads the way out of the cool office and into the sticky heat. She's almost as tall and thin as me, but her black ponytail is longer than mine and reaches her waist. She's wearing long black leggings

106

under her skirt and a black hoodie with the school logo over the polo shirt.

"Sooo, this is the canteen." Kiera points to an open area on the ground level. "Don't eat the burritos. They're absolutely vile. The *roti pratas* are good, and their *chicken rice* is okay." She waves at one of the dinner ladies, who grins and waves back. "Auntie Goh always gives me extra fries," she whispers.

On our way up the stairs, Sunitha's walking backwards ahead of me, while she explains the layout of the school. "We have most of our lessons in this building," she says. "But later today, we have third-language lessons, so I'll show you where the Danish classroom is in the morning break. Kiera has Mandarin as third language, and I have Dutch."

"Why Dutch?" I ask, before I can stop myself.

"I know, you're like me, you think she looks more French." Kiera giggles.

"*Moi?*" Sunitha says. "*Je suis* Dutch. Both my parents came to the Netherlands as Tamil refugees when they were kids. But we've lived in the US and Hong Kong before we came here."

"I'm like the apple that fell close to so many trees, it landed in the forest. I'm half French and half Irish and half Swiss and a little bit German," Kiera says. "And I'm totally boring because I've only ever lived here in Singapore."

"You can't be three halves, Kiera." Sunitha waves at an older, red-haired boy, who passes us in the hallway, then giggles behind her hand.

"How can you like that oaf, Sunitha?" Kiera rolls her eyes. "It's my youngest, incredibly annoying, older brother," she says to me. "I sooo wish water was thicker than blood in his case."

"What about you, Freja?" Sunitha asks.

It's the first time there's been a pause in their chatter, but I like them. "My mum's Danish, Dad's English, and I've never lived outside Denmark." Then, without knowing why, I add, "My stepmother's half English and half Chinese. Hong Kong Chinese." Clementine always stresses that.

They both nod, without asking questions. Being a mix is normal here. Not like in my small hometown in Denmark, where almost everyone is just Danish.

In the car to the airport in Copenhagen, Aunt Astrid kept telling me how fantastic it would be for me to experience Singapore's melting pot of cultures and religions. At the time, I thought she was only trying to cheer me up, but I'm beginning to think she might be right.

I wonder if Singapore was a melting pot when Ling was alive, and who her parents were. She looks Chinese, the sign on her grave is Chinese and she's buried in the pauper's section of a Chinese graveyard. But she speaks English, and if we're somehow related... She did say she remembered someone with yellow hair and blue eyes. Like Dad's. Like mine.

We're in a cool hallway, when a loud bell sounds. Students push past us, to and from lockers and classrooms.

"Come on," Sunitha says, "We'll find you a locker later."

Inside the classroom, the other kids flock around us. Before our form tutor arrives, most of them have told me their names and I've forgotten almost all of them again.

Sunitha pulls me onto a chair between her and Kiera.

"Can I sit next to Freja in Maths, then?" A girl called Cheryl Yi asks.

"It's freezing in here." Sunitha zips up her hoodie.

Kiera rolls her eyes. I think it's nice to come into the chill after the heat outside.

Ms Jones, our English and tutor group teacher, makes me stand up in front of everyone, which isn't as bad as I'd feared, because they're all so nice. I say my name and where I'm from and tell them I'll be here until next summer. Although, as soon as Mum's better, I'll be leaving.

After English and Maths and double Arts, it's lunch break. I'm sitting between Kiera, Cheryl Yi and Sunitha, with a crowd of boys and girls, up where I saw the monkey the other day. Everyone's chatting.

They ask me questions about Denmark and my old school. I'm not used to talking so much in a group. One of the things I've always liked about the scouts is that we do practical things together, and as long as you participate, no one notices if anything's wrong. It's easy to be invisible. But here they're listening and making me feel like I belong.

Sunitha nudges me, pulling me out of my thoughts. "We've all been the new kid," she says.

"Four times!" Cheryl Yi sighs.

"Except me and Sam and Rohaan." Kiera points at two boys I met in the morning.

"Oh, poor you," another boy says. Bits of food start flying around, after Kiera flips a crisp in his face. Behind us, less than two metres away, a hopeful monkey appears on the railing. I'm about to point, when I realize that this is normal.

"So, Singapore's your real home?" I ask Kiera.

She shrugs. "For me, home is wherever my heart actually is. When I'm in Ireland during the summer, that's my home. And when we visit my *grand-mère* in France and my uncle in Switzerland at Christmas, those places feel like home. The rest of the year, I guess, Singapore is kind of home."

"I'm not sure..." Sunitha pauses. "Amsterdam, I guess... I mean, that's where my grandparents and cousins are."

"When did you last live there?" I ask.

Sunitha counts on her fingers, mumbling. "We moved to the US when I was four, and to Hong Kong when I was seven, but then we lived in Amsterdam for one year when I was nine, before we moved here."

When I peek back over my shoulder, the monkey has gone. Instead, a boy is sitting there, leaning against the railing. His face is hidden behind his long black fringe and a thick book with a dragon on the cover.

It's Jason. I hadn't noticed him in class, and he wasn't one of the kids crowding around me this morning.

"Is Jason in our tutor group?" I whisper to Sunitha, when we're walking back to the classroom.

She nods.

"I feel bad for him," Kiera holds the door to the hallway for me. "His parents aren't here, and he's lost his best friend. It's sooo hard when your friends move back to Europe and forget about you."

"It's just as hard when you're the one who has to move." Sunitha shifts her school bag from one shoulder to the other.

"I've had sooo many friends move away. And I'm never ever the one to leave." Kiera sighs. "I know people who won't make friends with anyone who isn't here long term. They simply don't want to suffer the heartbreak." She glances sideways at me. "Don't worry, Freja, I'm not like that. I'm more of an if-there're-plenty-of-fish-in-the-sea-I-want-to-catch-all-of-them kind of person."

"That doesn't make any sense, Kiera," Sunitha says, snorting.

They chatter on, but I'm not listening any more. The whole morning, I've been busy and surrounded by people who want to be my friends. I haven't thought about Mum at all. What's even worse is that I've completely forgotten about Ling. The knots in my belly tighten. I want to be friends with Kiera and Sunitha and Cheryl Yi and the others, but first I have to find Ling and help her remember.

By the end of the school day, I'm exhausted by heat and newness. Although the classrooms are air-conditioned, in most breaks we're outside in the clammy heat. Everyone else is used to it. They don't even notice their damp polo shirts sticking to their backs.

After the last lesson, school buses are parked inside the school gates like plastic vehicles in a game of logic, waiting for someone to solve their traffic-jam puzzle. Kiera helps me find the minibus labelled *L1*. She lives two streets away from me, but she takes public transport with her big brothers because the school bus costs "a hand and a foot".

I almost automatically say "an arm and a leg", but I don't want to correct her. I'm only bilingual—Kiera must speak at least three languages, so it's understandable if she messes up a few phrases.

I'm the last person to squeeze inside the school bus, and the only empty seat is next to Jason.

"Hi," I say, when I sit down.

He glares at me and his lips twitch, before he turns away and leans against the window. That's what he does the whole way home, with his earphones plugged in. The volume's so loud I can hear buzzing voices speaking between peals of thunder, despite the rain which beats on the roof and cascades down the windows. The bus drops me off outside the gates to the house. Jason will be getting out in a moment too, but he doesn't even look up.

—23—

After unlocking the gate, I sprint across the empty drive-way through the downpour. My phone pings, and I stop on the veranda to read the message. It's from Aunt Astrid, saying how sorry she is that's she'd forgotten to send me a good luck message last night, and she hopes I've had a great first day. She also sends love from Mum.

One word stands out in the text: *forgotten*.

I haven't talked to Mum since I came to Singapore. They—Dad and Clementine, and possibly Aunt Astrid and perhaps Mum—believe it's best that way, but I'm not sure if it's best for Mum, or me, or any of us. Aunt Astrid had forgotten me. What if Mum forgets?

The house is quiet. When I drop my school bag with a plonk by the stairs, Maya comes out of the kitchen. She moves so silently in her bare feet that I only hear the soft swishes of her baggy printed trousers.

"How was school? You want a drink? And food to snack? Ma'am and the little ones are not home yet." She's all kindness and helpfulness, and that makes me miss Mum even more. I wish I could call Mum right now and tell her about my first day in school. Or Dad. But I'm not supposed to call him unless it's an emergency. Clementine isn't even here.

I follow Maya through the swing door into the kitchen. On the counter is a plate with sliced melon, papaya and pineapple, another with transparent rice-paper rolls containing salad and shredded carrot and shrimps, and a third with biscuits.

I gape at the generous spread. At home, I'd usually have a slice of bread with cheese and strawberry jam and a glass of milk. Or cordial if Mum had forgotten to buy milk.

"I don't know what snacks you want after school..." She finds a glass and asks me if I like watermelon juice.

I stay in the kitchen with Maya while she's chopping vegetables for dinner. Between mouthfuls, I tell her about the school and Kiera, Sunitha and Cheryl Yi. Talking distracts me from worrying about Ling. The thunderstorm's raging outside, so I can't go to the graveyard.

When Maya leaves to collect laundry upstairs, I take a look around the kitchen. The black-and-white tiles of the floor lead to a back door with a window to the driveway. From an open doorway next to the washing machine shines a purple light, through thin purple fabric. I wonder what's in there. I didn't notice it on the tour Clementine gave me the first evening.

I step nearer and lift the fabric aside. Inside is a small room with a miniature window. There's a tiny bed, fit for the smallest bear in *Goldilocks*—definitely too short for me—a chest of drawers, and a pinboard hidden behind layers of photos.

Everywhere else is covered in pink, purple, orange and red shawls with golden threads—even the lamps—transforming the tiny room into Aladdin's cave. Without the treasures.

When the kitchen door hinges squeak, I let the fabric fall and turn.

"Sorry. I didn't mean to..."

Maya smiles.

"D'you live in there?"

She nods and places the laundry basket by the washing machine, before she takes my hand and leads me inside.

"It's cosy. I like your... er... colours." The room's smaller than the bathroom I have to myself upstairs. My bed wouldn't even fit in here.

"I have my own window." She points at the small square, as if that's the room's best feature. "*Last time*, I live in a bomb shelter."

I'm searching for something to say, when I catch sight of the photos on the pinboard. "Who are they?" Almost all the photos are of children.

Her smile lights up the whole room, as she shows me a photo of a girl and a boy in blue school uniforms. "That is my Emilia. She is eight. And this is my angel, Raphael. He is seven in one month. And here are my nephews and nieces."

"So, where are they? Emilia and Raphael?" I ask.

"They live with my sister in the Philippines."

"All the time? But don't you miss them?"

She nods. "But I'm happy with such a nice family as this one, with sweet boys. And I send money home, so my children go to a good school. Sir gives me a ticket home for my birthday and Christmas and summer, so I see my babies three times in one year."

"Aren't you afraid they'll forget you?"

"No," she says, without a hint of doubt.

"But what if... what if you forget them?"

"Never! I can never forget them. They are here..." She taps the pinboard. "And here," she says, placing a hand on her heart.

Afterwards, the kitchen seems too big and colourless. Maya is washing salad, and I'm drinking the last of the watermelon juice, when the gates to the street open with metallic creaks. Outside, white reversing lights beam through the glittering raindrops. Maya wipes her hands.

"Thank you, Maya." I surprise myself by giving her a hug.

"Tell me what you want to snack after school, and I have it ready for you," she says. But from the way she hugs me back, I think she understands that I'm not only thanking her for the food.

A moment later, she's by the car, with a large umbrella, opening the door for Clementine, then carrying the twins, one after the other, into the house. Both boys are whinging.

I pick up my school bag.

"They're hungry, Maya. But please don't give them anything sweet before dinner."

"No, ma'am," Maya says from the dining table, where she's already placed the twins in their high chairs.

Clementine inspects the leather soles of her high-heeled sandals. "Awful. Just awful. I thought I could get home before the rain, but the moment it started, PIE was one big traffic jam."

Maya's in the kitchen, the boys are wailing, and I don't know what to say.

"Did you have a nice day in school, Freja?" Clementine asks, while she scrolls down the feed on her phone.

"Yes," I answer, before I tell her I have homework.

In my room, I open the window and peer out through the sheets of rain. A flash of lightning splits the sky. Something Maya said nudges my memory. She said she had a room without a window at her last family—just like Ling remembered waking up next to her mother in a windowless room. What if Ling's mother was a nanny or a helper like Maya?

Perhaps she met a man with yellow hair through the family, fell in love and had Ling. But why would she then continue to be a nanny, with Ling sleeping by her side? Why would Ling end up forgotten in the pauper's section of the graveyard?

—24—

The next two days, Kiera, Sunitha and Cheryl Yi lead me in and out of classrooms, up and down stairs, from *chicken rice* to *roti prata*. All three of them ask me over to their houses after school, but I can't just forget about Ling. I want to be home if she returns, and ready for any opportunity to visit the graveyard if she doesn't.

I rush to the bus when the bell rings, so I can avoid sitting next to Jason. We still haven't said a word to each other, and it's starting to feel weird. I don't know if he doesn't want to talk to me because I'll be moving away again soon or because of the offering, or something I said when I visited him.

Like clockwork, on the way home from school, thunderstorms erupt and hurl water towards the ground. Claps of thunder boom so often, the dark sky rumbles constantly above the blinking flashes.

After I've eaten Maya's snacks, I say I have homework, to get away from Clementine and the twins. Then I sit at my desk by the window and doodle in my exercise books, trying to spot Lizzie in the room or Ling outside. I wish I could go to the graveyard to search for her, but lightning makes it unsafe to go into the forest. It's not that I mind the rain.

Outside on the landing, the twins keep asking, "Where Frej-ja?" and Maya shushes them and tells them not to disturb me.

I can't avoid Clementine and the twins at dinner time, but that's not too bad. The boys are sitting safely in their high chairs. I even help cut their food into tiny squares, and happily give Eddie the broccoli on my plate, after he asks for more "trees".

When I ask Clementine how old the house is, she guesses it's from the 1980s. So Ling can't have lived here.

"Obviously it's been completely renovated a few years ago," she says and begins to tell me everything she would do differently if they were to refurbish it now.

"What kind of houses did people live in a hundred years ago?" I ask.

"That depends on who you were." She wipes Billy and Eddie's hands, while Maya clears the table. "Many lived in huts or shacks in *kampongs*, or squeezed together in small upstairs rooms of the shophouses. Those who were well-off lived in the black-and-white bungalows, like the ones we drove past on the way to the beach."

"And did the rich people have Chinese helpers or nannies back then?" I ask, when the kitchen door has closed behind Maya.

"I'm sure they did. I had a Chinese *amah*, while I was growing up. Is this for a school project?"

"Uh huh." I feel only the slightest flutter of guilt at the lie.

On Wednesday evening, there's an information meeting about our school trip to a Malaysian island in October. When we arrive at the school, Kiera comes running and drags me, with Clementine close behind, over to meet her mum. Until the meeting starts, Clementine's chatting with Kiera's mum and Sunitha's and Cheryl Yi's parents, as if she were my mum.

"I'm glad you've found such nice friends," she says later in the evening, on her way upstairs to check on the twins. "Kiera's mum wanted you to come for a sleepover this weekend... And did you know Cheryl Yi is in the girl guides? I'm sure she'd love to take you along to a meeting."

"Let's see," I say.

The moment I enter my room, I smell bonfire smoke. I shut the door, while my eyes flick to the closed window. Ling's sitting on the window seat.

"Ling!" I lower my voice and whisper, "I'm so glad you're back. What happened? Where did you go?"

"Somewhere else. I got lost and could not find the banyan tree for a while."

"A while? It was days ago..."

"Was it?" Ling shrugs, as if four days means nothing. "Then I thought I remembered where I used to live... but a *getai* distracted me. Afterwards, when I tried to find the house, I could not remember where to go."

"The house with the windowless room? I've been thinking... Could your mum have been a nanny or a helper?"

"I do not know." She follows me into the bathroom.

"Is this only for you?" she asks, wide-eyed. "I remember standing in a queue to use the toilet... but that was another place. Another windowless room with other people. Oh, I remember how Ma cried herself to sleep every night."

I stop in the middle of brushing my teeth. "My mum used to cry herself to sleep. Sometimes when I came and snuggled up to her during the night her pillow was wet. And so was Dad's. I can't remember why they were crying. Perhaps it was after granddad died. Why did your Mum cry?"

Ling shrugs again. When I pull off my clothes and get into the shower, she sits down on my laundry basket. Lizzie flitters up the wall behind her.

The water drums on my head. I think back to a day with rain clouds inside the house. I remember hiding in the small space under the terrace. Sunshine filtered through the cracks between the boards onto my green trainers.

While I'm detangling my hair, I tell Ling about that day.

"I must've been six because I got those trainers in first grade. Suddenly, there was a girl next to me. She had dark curly hair and brown eyes. 'If we sing a song, we can't hear the crying,' she said. 'And you don't have to think it's your fault.'

"When all was quiet, we made tea and cakes in our den out of dandelions we picked on the overgrown lawn. A little later, Mum came outside. She couldn't get under the terrace, but she lay down on her stomach and watched us play. 'Oh, how I've missed hearing your voice, *skat*.' She smiled with her red-rimmed eyes. *Skat* means treasure in Danish, and that's what she usually calls me. Dad used to call me his blue titmouse."

She missed my voice? How long hadn't I been talking? Days? Weeks?

"Treasure," Ling says. "I like that. What was the other girl called?"

"Mum suggested I call her Gullveig. 'It's from Norse mythology and believed to be another name for Freja,' Mum said. She went along with everything, set four places at the table and tucked Gullveig in at night, even though Dad was against it. He didn't like my imaginary friend."

"So this girl was not real?"

I shake my head. "I didn't realize it at the time." We go back into my room, and I crawl under the duvet. "Dad thinks you're imaginary too."

"I'm sorry. I called your father into the garden. I hoped he could see me."

"You made him sleepwalk? He never saw you, but I think maybe he dreamt about you."

"Sorry," she says again, and settles in the bed next to me. "I have stopped calling him."

—25—

Ling tells me that during the day, when I'm in school, she returns to the little grove. To her gravestone. She doesn't like the sun or too much light, and there are offerings in the cemetery she can feed on. She wanders the streets at night, while I'm sleeping, searching for the house, her old home. It's an impossible task—all she remembers is a windowless room.

By Friday afternoon, I'm beginning to panic. Tomorrow there's only a week until the end of the Hungry Ghost Festival. If we can't find out who she was before next Saturday, then Ling must return to the realm of the dead, unremembered.

She's lying on my bed, stroking the pink bedspread with both hands. Her black hair fans out around her head.

"I wish I could touch this softness," she says. I'm not sure she's talking about the bed or the fabric. To jog her memory, I ask her who taught her Morse code and question her about that windowless room, her mum and why she felt the need to check if it was safe to go into the nursery. Nothing helps.

When I run out of questions, I flop down on the bed next to Ling to rest a moment. But, like the last few nights, or whenever I close my eyes, visions of the wildfire appear. The red-orange light of the sky-high flames fill my mind. I can't erase the image, and I can't think of a way to smother the fire. Even if there isn't a *feng shui* link between the fire—the red colour in the north-west—and Ling's missing memories, I wish we could save the white tiger.

My phone rings. While I rummage through my school bag to find it, I wonder who it might be. Dad has called me every night from whichever M-city he's in, but he's coming home today, so it can't be him. Clementine has taken the twins to a play date, and I'm not answering if it's her.

The number's unknown but begins with +45, so I know it's from Denmark.

"*Hallo,*" I say in Danish.

"*Hi,* skat!"

"Mum!"

"*I've missed you so much!*" She tells me she's feeling better, and that it helps to talk to outsiders. I want to ask if she talks about me, but I don't.

It's a voice call. She says her connection isn't good enough for video, but I think that's a fib. It's much easier to lie to people if they can't see your eyes. At least it works both ways.

"*How's the house? And your room? I want to know everything.*"

"It's great." Suddenly, I don't know what to tell Mum. The room's much bigger than my room at home. All the furniture is new. I don't want to tell her that Clementine has bought me lots of clothes and that Dad gave me the phone I've begged her for since before Christmas. It might make her sad if she believes I'm better off being here than at home. And I definitely don't want her to worry that I like Clementine. But I also don't want her to know that Dad has left me here and gone on a business trip—that might make her upset. And I can't tell her how much I miss her, as that will only make her cry.

I try to describe everything in a neutral tone.

"*And the... the little boys?*" Mum asks.

"They're okay. Cute, I guess. Billy's rather bossy. Eddie's quieter, except when he wants someone to read to him." I smile, recalling how he kept asking, "Again, Frej-ja?" with a puppy face.

"*You read to them?*" There's an unusual tightness to Mum's voice.

"Only once. In the car. I don't want... I don't have time to play with them."

Mum sounds normal when she asks if Clementine's nice to me.

"Really nice," I say. "Obviously not as nice as you, Mum."

"*It's okay*, skat," she says. "*I want her to be nicer than me, because I haven't*—" Mum's voice breaks into a sob.

I hurry to change the subject and tell her about my new school and friends. She likes the sound of them. And I love the sound of her voice and especially her giggles, when I report some of the funny things Kiera says.

After we hang up, I sit for a while, staring at the phone. Mum hadn't forgotten me, just like I hadn't forgotten her. But it's strange, being on opposite sides of the world and in different time zones. When I'm awake and it's the middle of the night in Denmark, it sometimes feels like we're not even living in the same universe.

"Who was that?" Ling asks. "You look happy, but I did not understand a word you said."

"My mum." I can't help smiling. She seems so much better.

It gives me new energy and determination. Despite the dangers, we must return to the world with the mythical creatures.

"We have to free the white tiger," I say out loud. "Perhaps we can use the net of lianas to pull it out... I just wish there was a way to save the forest." I try to explain the idea of a link between the red fire in the north-west and Ling's memory loss. It sounds mad and far-fetched, so I turn my focus back to more practical matters. "It's not like the black tortoise can bring us water from the lake, is it?"

"No, the tortoise cannot help us," Ling says. "We need rain."

It's pouring down outside. But in the mythical world there wasn't a single cloud in sight.

"Are you suggesting we bring rain clouds along through the banyan tree?"

"Of course not," Ling says. "But we could ask the dragon for help."

There are so many things wrong with that sentence, I list them, counting them out on my fingers. "One: how are we supposed to find a dragon? Two: how can we ask him? Three: why would he do what we ask him? Four: dragon's usually spew fire, not rain. And five: have you gone mad?"

Ling giggles. "You are funny," she says. "I am talking about a Chinese dragon, not one of your western fairy-tale creatures." Then she's suddenly serious. "I remember hiding behind a chair and listening to stories about dragons and princesses."

"What kind of chair? Close your eyes. Tell me what you see."

"Er... A small rattan chair next to a big one."

"What else?" Eagerly, I move to sit on a corner of the bed. The weave of the pink bedspread is visible through Ling's thin arm.

After a while, she says, "Yellow hair."

I close my eyes and try to imagine what she's seeing. It's like I'm remembering something similar. I'm sitting behind a chair, but it's a rocking chair, not a rattan chair. Tufts of Dad's yellow hair stick out through gaps in the chair's high back. He's rocking, while he's speaking in a low, soothing voice. I wonder why I'm sitting behind the chair instead of on his lap, if he's reading me a bedtime story.

"A man's voice," Ling says.

"Reading to you or someone else?"

"I do not know. Perhaps both."

Perhaps both. A shiver makes my shoulders tense up. To evade the rocking-chair memory, I ask, "And you think the dragon can extinguish that wildfire?"

Ling nods. "And then, when all the red is gone, I will remember everything."

Her eyes shine with a new-found hope I don't want to snuff out. Dad isn't landing from his M-city until later tonight. Clementine and the twins aren't home yet.

"Okay," I say, "let's go." I pull on my long combat trousers and check I have my Swiss Army knife, the compass and the map with the white folds. My phone's almost out of battery, but it won't work where we're going anyway, so I leave it in the charger.

Ling's already waiting in the garden, when I unfurl the rope. I take a last look around the room. I have a feeling of being unprepared, like there's a vital piece of equipment I've forgotten. While I'm running up the road after Ling, with the root rope slapping against my thigh, I realize that my keys are still in my school bag.

—26—

Once we're inside the hushed den, I hesitate.

"You have to take my hand as soon as you feel solid, okay?" Getting separated from Ling is one of many parts of our plan that could go wrong. Chief among them is my fear that the flames have engulfed the banyan tree, so we'll be going from the frying pan into an actual fire. No amount of preparation could help us out of that situation.

"Can you picture the mythical world?"

Ling nods, and I don't doubt her. My own memories of that place are vivid.

After we start running, I shout, "We wish to return to the vermillion bird and the white tiger and the wildfire!" The banyan tree should have no doubts about our destination.

Before I know it, we're spinning. My hair escapes the scrunchy and whips my face. I'm pressed against the root cage, with my eyes closed and the eerie sounds of the dead in my ears, when Ling clutches my hand. She keeps on squeezing, until we stop moving and all is quiet. And cool. The tree is unharmed!

It doesn't take long to discover that so are the eastern and southern parts of the island. North and west of us, though, the forest is ablaze. But at least the flames haven't yet reached our grassy hill.

"Come," Ling says. "We must go east."

We run down the hill until the rainforest slows our progress. This time, I'm in front, holding my compass, and Ling's the one struggling to keep up.

We're jogging through the dense greenery, when we hear a high-pitched wail nearby.

"Is that a baby?" It can't be the vermillion bird. I veer off course, in the direction of the sound.

"Wait, Freja."

But I won't wait. The sound reminds me of something. Of some time, long ago. Someone was crying, and I ignored it.

The baby cries again, but now the sound is much further away. I speed up.

"Wait," Ling calls again from behind, "I cannot run any more."

The next muted cry is so distant, I can't tell where it's coming from. I stop and wait for Ling.

We're standing in a grove of banana trees. The large oval leaves make a shady canopy between the pole-like trunks. Ling picks bananas from one of the low-hanging clusters that are hanging upside down above our heads. We sink against two trunks, sitting across from each other, tearing banana skins off and eating the ripe mush inside the small bananas in two bites. This will give us energy.

"I never thought I would taste anything ever again. Bananas used to be my favourite food!" Ling beams, with a happy smile shining out of her eyes.

"You're remembering something. That's good."

She stares off into the distance. "There were banana trees behind the house. And a boy with hair like just-ripe bananas. Like yours."

"And the house... Do you remember the house? Did it have black-and-white striped blinds?" That would confirm my theory that she lived in one of the colonial bungalows and her mother was a maid.

Ling nods.

In the silence, we hear the cry far, far away. My legs are tired. I'm full in a good way. Mixed with the aroma of bananas is a peachy fragrance, like the scent of the frangipani trees in Dad's garden at night. But it isn't night and I can't see any of the exotic flowers or any peach trees.

I inhale, then almost retch. A light breeze carries a disgusting smell of rotten food, like an overfull rubbish bin on a hot summer's day. Now, I have no problem getting up. Is it the smell of the vermillion bird? Has the bird taken the child, carrying it off, like a stork would carry a baby?

"Come on! We have to find that baby." I pull Ling to her feet.

"Have you seen my baby?" a musical voice asks.

Coming towards us, weaving her way through the banana trees, is the most beautiful woman I've ever seen. Like an Asian Snow White, her lips are blood-red and her hair falls in long, ebony-black, shining waves, which would make

Clementine envious. Her long dress is white as snow, as if she's stepped out of a detergent ad, instead of appearing from behind a banana tree in the middle of a rainforest.

Ling clasps my hand, as if she's afraid.

"Do you know where my baby is?" the woman asks again.

"We heard it cry. But it's really far away." I want Ling to let go of my hand so I'm ready if the woman needs me to give her a hug.

"Did the vermillion bird take your baby?" I ask.

"That terrible bird," she mutters. Tears drip from her long lashes. "First it sets the forest on fire, and now it has kidnapped my baby."

In searching for the baby, I'd almost forgotten about the fire.

"We'll help you, right, Ling?"

Ling nods slowly, reluctantly.

"That is very kind of you." The woman comes close to me. The smell of overripe peaches is strong. She smiles and raises a hand towards my face. Then she strokes my cheek— not with her fingers, but with the tips of her pointed nails. It sends a shiver down my back. I feel a trickle on my cheek and wipe it away, thinking it's one of her tears. But the smear across my fingers is red.

"Come this way," she says briskly, before she turns and strides back in the direction she came from.

Ling hesitates. "We should not go with her," she whispers, as I pull her along through the banana grove. "There are stories... someone used to tell me—"

"I'm glad you're remembering," I say. Right now, helping the woman seems far more important.

At the edge of the grove, the woman stops and retrieves a net of lianas that have been knotted together with exceptional skill. "I shall catch the bird and save my baby," she says.

"Who are you?" I'm impressed she's so well prepared.

"You can call me Pontiana. Some people do." She smiles and gazes at me with Mum's eyes. The same love, the same twinkle, the exact same colour. Then I blink, and Pontiana's irises are as dark as her pupils. I wonder how I could have thought her eyes were grey-green like Mum's.

"What do you need us to do?" I ask.

"The fire has gotten out of control." Pontiana brushes a stray leaf off her dress, which is still white and crisp. "Only one thing can stop it now. A tropical rainstorm."

"We were going to find the dragon..." Ling says.

"That is wonderfully clever, dearest."

Ling blushes.

"The azure dragon will come once he understands the vermillion bird is responsible for the inferno. The two have a history of strife. Let him know he can find her by the banyan tree on the hill." Pontiana speaks in a sugar-coated voice that's impossible to resist.

"But don't you need our help to save your baby from the bird first?" I ask.

Pontiana responds with a little laugh that sounds like chiming bells, before she leans towards me and kisses my forehead. The spot her lips touch burns like I've been stung by a wasp.

"You are deliciously sweet, my dear," she says. Without another word she strolls south, with the net of lianas over her shoulder.

"She doesn't seem to be like us. Like me. A real human," I whisper.

Ling shakes her head. "There was one story about a woman in a grove of banana trees and the scent of night flowers... Oh, I wish I could remember..."

"Who told you? Your mum?" I'm thinking about my own mum and her happy smile in the beach photo I found in Dad's office. I still can't remember that day, but I think I remember a time when she wasn't sad.

"I used to run after Ma through the house, from the nursery and downstairs to the kitchen. The Malay cook would lift me up to sit on her lap. She is the one who told me stories, while Ma washed the sheets." Ling rubs her eyes. "Come. We must find the dragon."

We jog and run and walk through the rainforest for hours. Twice, we swim across lazy rivers. I keep checking my compass to make sure we're heading south-east. When we reach the shore, we stand on the empty beach, breathing the salty air, scanning the horizon.

White-capped waves churn under the clear sky. Faraway islands, like green boils, interrupt the blue perfection. Parallel to the shore, a set of three spectacular arches curve in and out of the sea. Their brightness is blinding.

"Dragon!" Ling calls. "Esteemed dragon. We request a favour."

The arches shift direction and flow towards us, fluidly, as if they're made entirely of water. As it approaches, the metallic blue-green scales that are reflecting the sunlight become distinguishable, and I can make out the shape of the creature.

I'm staring, trying to grasp how this can possibly be a dragon. It looks more like a giant sea serpent, perhaps the

Midgard Serpent in Norse mythology, who will bring about the end of the world.

I want to run as far from the shore as possible, but Ling walks into the sea, smiling, like it's her lucky day.

When a huge head slides out of the water right next to her, she giggles and pats it, as if it was a puppy. Like a dog, the dragon sticks its tongue out. Unlike a dog's, the dragon's tongue is longer than Ling's waist-length hair.

Gingerly, I wade after Ling.

The long snake-like neck rises further out of the sea. A million deep-blue fish scales gleam. The dragon dips its head, tipping its stag antlers towards me in a polite greeting. I rub it behind its fluffy, tea-cosy-sized ears, while I try to decide if the head itself more resembles a cow's or a camel's.

"Venerable dragon. The forest in the north-west of the island is burning. We need a rainstorm to extinguish the blaze." Ling goes on to tell him that the vermillion bird started the fire, but that we expect she's been captured by now and taken to the hill with the banyan tree.

At the mention of the vermillion bird, the eyes of the dragon darken. The skin above the bump between them contracts.

"Could you perhaps drop us off on the hill, esteemed dragon, before you... er... unleash the... torrents?" I ask, remembering at the last minute to speak in the same respectful tone and formal language as Ling.

The dragon bows again. Out of the water, he pulls a bird-like leg with a clawed foot and lifts first Ling, then me, up onto the second of the three arches that curve out of the surface. I copy Ling and lie down, wrapping my legs and arms around his neck.

With a forceful push-off, the dragon frees himself from the water. He doesn't have any wings, but moves through the air with the same smooth wave-like motion as he swam in the sea. The scales are too bright to look at directly and extremely slippery. Every rise causes us to glide backwards, while the falls make us slide forward.

At first my eyes are closed, but soon I get used to the rhythm of his flight and stop worrying about falling. Ling is tittering and squealing in front of me. Below lies the blue sea and, on one side, an endless ocean. On the other side, smoke from the fire chokes the red-glowing island beneath a blanket of grey haze.

The dragon stays above the water, following the coastline south of Singapore. I wonder if he has misunderstood us and is taking us somewhere else. But when I glance back over my shoulder, I see what's behind us. At the end of his tail, wispy white threads are pulling ever-growing clouds along.

After we have circled the whole island, he spirals towards its centre. The swelling ring of clouds fill the sky, and darken. The wind rises. Holding on is getting more and more difficult.

It's a relief when the dragon hovers near the ground to let us slide down. We're at the bottom of the hill, where the tiger emerged. Everything has become hazy. Smoke billows around us. Cracks and sizzles from a thousand campfires advance towards us. The rainforest moans.

While we're running up towards the tree, to get under cover, it begins to rain. Behind us, the azure dragon flies faster and faster in circles above the wildfire.

The wind tears at us. I notice the pit and grab hold of Ling, in time to stop her from falling into the gaping hole. The white tiger looks up at us and growls, before it resumes licking its fur. It isn't alone.

The vermillion bird, trussed up in a net of lianas, cowers next to the tiger. On the bird's other side, and bigger even than the tiger, lies a giant black tortoise.

The liana net Pontiana used to capture the bird resembles the grass-woven net used to camouflage the pit. It makes me wonder if Pontiana has trapped all three creatures. But why would she do that?

Leaves and twigs swirl around us. I can't see Pontiana anywhere. I can't even make out the banyan tree, through the torrents.

"I thought it would just rain," I shout.

"The Chinese words for tornado mean 'dragon twisting wind'," Ling yells back.

Fighting to move forward in the wind, we creep uphill on hands and feet, towards the tree. It's the nearest place to seek cover.

When I detect Ling isn't next to me, I pause. She's sitting back on her knees, grinning from ear to ear, with rain sliding down over her closed eyes and hair whipping wildly around her head.

"I remember," she yells. Behind her, the red glow has dulled to a weaker orange. "I remember William. My brother. The boy with banana-yellow hair. He called me 'beloved sister'."

At that moment, it feels like something clears in my head. I have the weirdest sensation: my mind has been transformed into a loft full of memory boxes, and I'm standing on a ladder, looking at them. Some are small, transparent and accurately tagged: *Canoe trip to Sweden*; *Seeing the newborn twins in London*; *Easter scouting camp*. Bigger, half-open boxes contain jumbles of memories. They're labelled things like: *Mum*; *Dad*; *Beach days*; *Tree climbing*. At the far end of the gabled space, weak light shines through cracks in a tiny, grimy window. A dusty ray hits a box completely covered by cobwebs.

As I'm watching, a gust of wind sweeps through the loft. The flaps of the open boxes flutter. A few threads of the cobweb snap. The wind lifts the right-hand bottom corner of the tangled web, revealing an animal letter. An alligator. Drawn in pencil, without colour. It looks gloomy.

Suddenly I'm certain that whatever's in the box is the reason Mum's unhappy. Is it me? The box could be labelled 'FREJA'.

"Come on, Ling!" I hold my hand out to her. I have to leave this place, before the cobweb is swept away and frees the flaps of the box.

Lightning flashes behind us. Ling's too far away to reach and too light. She doesn't stand a chance against the gale. I throw back one end of the root-rope and yell at her to hold on. Together we make it up to the tree. I'm fighting the urge to peep at the hidden box as much as I'm fighting the storm.

"It's not safe here," I say, when we're leaning against the trunk. The wind howls and sweeps through the gaps between the roots, all the way into my mind. I take her hand.

"But the fire is dying, the north-west is less red. I am remembering." Ling holds me back. "William promised he would never forget—"

"Lightning might strike the tree," I say, and tug at her. "And then... And then we'd be stuck." I'm so scared, I'm shaking. I hope she's remembered enough for us to discover who she was, but even if she hasn't, I can't stay. "Please, Ling. Please, let's go."

She gazes at me, and I think she sees the storm behind my eyes, because she nods and pulls me into a run.

My last thought before we start spinning is that I hope the box never opens. Whatever's inside must be something I don't want to ever remember.

—28—

We emerge into a dark, starless evening. On the walk back to the house, I try to come up with a way to get into the garden without my key. Anything to avoid thinking about the box under the cobwebs.

Ling floats alongside me, telling me things she's remembering about her brother, William.

"... Blue eyes. The soft patter of his feet across the nursery floor early in the morning, while it was still dark. The feeling of his hand when he took mine and we ran through the garden. His voice when he read me stories and taught me to read and write. He was the best brother in the world."

"D'you remember your surname?" I pant.

Ling's silent for a moment before she answers, "No."

The car stands in the driveway, so Clementine must be home. I stop on the pavement outside. "What was your father's name?"

"I... I called him 'Sir'." Her eyes fill with tears. "I do not remember his name."

"Don't worry. It'll come to you."

"He looked like your father, except for his white clothes. Sir always wore white."

"Perhaps he was a doctor."

"Doctor..." Ling mutters. "Someone was always asking for the doctor."

As I'm trying to climb the fence at the back of the garden, I wonder if we left the mythical world too early; if Ling remembers enough. If we'll be forced to return.

I shiver. My skin crawls with a clutter of spiders. They're dispersing, tearing at the cobweb that's hiding the memory box. I'll do anything to avoid going back.

Ling wants to pull me up, but here in the real world my hand slides right through hers. I wish she could hold on to something, so she could fetch my house key.

After I've given up, I press the buzzer, hoping Maya will be letting me in.

No such luck. Before the buzzing noise has stopped, Clementine opens the front door.

"Where have you been? I tried to call you," she screeches. "You can't leave the house without telling anyone! You're not in a Danish village."

Ling flees around the corner of the house.

"Sorry," I mutter. "I just went for a walk, and I left my phone so it could charge."

"A walk? You're drenched and completely muddy. It isn't even raining." She wrinkles her nose. "And it smells like you've been to a bonfire."

"I said I'm sorry." I sit down on the veranda steps, with my back to Clementine, to untie my mud-caked hiking boots.

"You went to Bukit Brown, didn't you?"

The double knot on one of my boots is so wet it's impossible to loosen. I take my knife out, unfold the screwdriver and bore it into the lump. "It really isn't dangerous," I reply, although I'm not so sure any more.

"That's not the point. We told you to stay away from the cemetery."

"*You* told me," I say under my breath. The knot has come undone, and I put the knife down to untie the laces.

"Is that a knife? Don't tell me you're running around Singapore with a weapon." Clementine bends and picks up my Swiss Army knife. "That could get us all in trouble with the authorities."

"It's not a weapon."

"I'll have to talk to your daddy about this. From now on it stays in your room." She drops my knife on the veranda before she points at my hiking boots. "And leave those outside," she says, turning away.

I untie the tree-root rope from my waist and dump it next to the veranda. She won't want that in the house either. I'm brushing the worst of the dirt off my combat trousers, when Clementine screams. It's a high-pitched, ear-splitting scream, which morphs into the word "snake". She's pointing at the driveway, while trying to pull me into the house.

The twins come running from the sofa, one of them with a remote control in his little hand. She lets go of me to block their way and screams for them to get back. Eddie begins wailing.

"It's not a snake," I call above the din, picking up the root-rope I left next to the veranda. In the dim light, it actually does resemble the striped bronzeback I saw at the zoo. "It's just an aerial root from a tree." I hold it towards Clementine in my smudged green and brown hand. "And if it was a bronzeback, then they're not venomous."

"Get. That. Out." Clementine's staring from the root to my face.

"Rooooot," Billy says, stretching his arms towards me. "Frej-ja, want root!"

"No, Billy. It's dirty," she says in a tone I haven't heard before, and she yanks both of them back to the lounge. "Freja, take those filthy trousers and socks off down here. I don't want you to drag dirt all over the house."

Without a word, I comply. *"I don't want you to drag dirt all over the house."* That's exactly what Mum used to say. Although I can't remember when she last said it. Lately, she didn't care much if the floor was a bit mucky, and I'd been doing most of the hoovering.

After folding the front of my T-shirt up, I use it to carry the stuff from my pockets upstairs.

When I close the door to my room, I hiss, "You're not my mother."

—29—

"My brother used to have a stepmother, too," Ling says. She's standing on my desk, glowing faintly in the unlit room. "She was kind to him, but not to me."

"What d'you mean?" I unfurl the T-shirt and unload my stuff on the bed. "Wasn't your mum his stepmother?"

"No."

There's a series of quiet knocks on my door, and Maya enters.

"Ma'am said for you to shower before you eat." She places a tray with sandwiches and a glass of milk on the desk where Ling stood a moment ago. Then she takes a chocolate bar from the pocket of her wide trousers, puts it next to the plate and winks at me.

After I've thanked Maya, and she's gone, Ling floats back inside, through the wall, although the window's open. I swallow one of the tuna-salad triangles—I'm starving— before I step into the shower. Ling sits in the sink, while I'm scrubbing my dirty nails and shampooing my hair.

I'm trying to detangle the strands, with Ling gazing over my shoulder into the mirror, when I notice three thin lines on my cheek. They're deeper than the scratches on my hands, and perfect, parallel lines. I must've run right through a bush with long thorns.

"I don't understand..." I pull on my pyjamas before I'm completely dry, wrap my hair in a towel and grab another sandwich. "How could this William be your half-brother if your mum wasn't his stepmother?"

"Ma was William's nursemaid. His mother died when he was born. Ma said Sir was grief-stricken afterwards."

I push the food away. In my notebook, I begin to make a list of everything we've discovered, starting with Ling's brother and his blue eyes.

Ling hugs her knees and leans back into the pillows on the window seat. When I stop writing, she goes on talking. "Ma took care of William and tried to console Sir. She said that once, only once, on William's third birthday, Sir drank too much, and she consoled him too much. She said he did not remember it afterwards. She never told him he was my father."

"But that's awful. Your poor mum. Wouldn't your dad have been happy to know he had a daughter?"

"I have been watching your father and your stepmother... but it was different in my time. A taboo. Ma was already shunned because she was pregnant. She did not want anyone to suspect the father was a Westerner, so she made up a story about a secret engagement to a recently dead Chinese servant in a neighbouring household. We all believed her—I looked like Ma not like Sir."

"So how did you find out?"

"Ma was crying. Someone was screaming at her." Ling closes her eyes. "I do not quite remember."

"William must have known too, if he called you... beloved sister." I stumble over the words. They sound too formal, like something you'd write on a gravestone, not say out loud. But I guess they spoke differently in the past.

Ling smiles, but like a flash of lightning it's followed by thunder. "He cannot have meant it. He forgot about me. I hoped and hoped; it was all I had, after Ma died..."

"Were you still in the black-and-white house?" I ask, to stop her from crying.

"No. Ma and I shared a dark room with six other women, in the Pagoda Street block. Ma was ill and coughed constantly. They all did. On her good days, she talked about William and his father. She loved them both. 'William is a good boy,' she said. She was certain he would find me and take care of me. She was wrong.

"The coffin-makers and tombstone-carvers in Macao Street gave me coins to help them with English spelling. After Ma died, when I began coughing up blood myself, they did not want me near their shops. Until I stopped going outside, I looked for William everywhere, but I never saw him. He never came back. He forgot he ever had a sister."

"I'm sure he didn't."

A breeze rattles the flaps on my memory loft, as if Ling's newfound memories should make me want to peek in the hidden box.

"Your last memories are so concrete... street names and everything. Perhaps the dragon has the fire under control and

147

it's all coming back. Do you remember the surname now? Or the street from when you lived with William?"

She shakes her head, then hides her face in her palms. I can see her tears through her hands.

"I have an idea. You remember the house itself, right?"

We try to draw the house.

I'm drawing, as Ling's describing windows, the veranda, the roof and the striped blinds. The result looks like something I could've drawn when I was six. But it's clearly a black-and-white bungalow.

"Clementine told me the black-and-whites are listed, so the one you lived in might still be here. Can you search for it during the night? If we have an address, we might be able to find out who lived in the house. And perhaps seeing it will make more of your memories come back."

At a hard knock, Ling ducks under the bed. Dad swings my door open.

"Why are you sitting in the dark?" he says and turns on the ceiling lamp.

He gives me a hug, moves my food tray to the window seat and leans against the desk across from me. Lizzie hangs from the ceiling above his head. I'm about to show her to him, when he begins speaking.

"Freja," he says. "I understand it's difficult for you... coming here... not knowing how Mum's doing... starting a new school... me travelling..."

And I know what's coming. He's going to tell me off for going to the cemetery and carrying my knife.

"... But I must say, I'm a bit disappointed," he continues, in a voice that clearly means it's more than a bit. "Clementine's making such an effort, and you're not even trying. She says you mope in your room every afternoon—"

"I have homework."

"And evening. I doubt you have that much homework." He takes my hand. "You're part of this family. We want you to be part of this family. Please try."

I'm staring down at our hands. My right thumb still has a tinge of green-brown from the root-rope. It makes me think of the hidden box. Does Dad know what it contains?

"She also says the mum of one of your new friends called to invite you over, but you don't want to go—"

"I just didn't want to go that day!"

Kiera, Sunitha and Cheryl Yi have plans to browse around Chinatown tomorrow. I said I wasn't sure I could come, because Dad wasn't arriving home until tonight. But now that I know Ling used to live in Chinatown... Perhaps I can uncover something helpful. And it's the perfect excuse to get out of Clementine's family-time.

"Is it okay if I hang out with some girls from school tomorrow?" I ask.

"Of course it is." Dad smiles. "I'm glad you've found friends already." He gives me another hug and leaves, without mentioning my knife or Bukit Brown.

"Why are you not trying to be part of the family?" Ling asks from under the bed. She floats up through the mattress to lie on the pink bedspread. "Is your stepmother evil?"

"No." I say, "That's the problem. Clementine's nice. Most of the time. Too nice. But she already has Dad and the twins."

"She is lucky," Ling says.

149

I nod. "Mum only has me. If I end up really liking Clementine... If I become part of her happy family... then my mum would be all alone."

"Why? Would you not still love her?"

"Of course. But..." I don't know if I can explain to Ling why it would feel like a betrayal. "The day I realized that we wouldn't ever be a family again, I was eight, almost nine. Mum said Dad wanted me to meet someone and that her name was Clementine. I remember the first thought that went through my head was that if I ever wanted to name a girl after a fruit, then I'd prefer 'Apple' because apples grow in Denmark."

"But mandarin oranges are auspicious," Ling says.

"She's not called 'Mandarin', though, is she?"

Ling shrugs.

"I said I didn't want to meet his stupid girlfriend... and that's when Mum told me Clementine was pregnant and they were getting married. Dad was starting a new family. As if it was as easy as starting a new drawing!" I rip my sketch of the black-and-white house from the notebook, crumple it up and throw it in the bin.

"Mum said it wouldn't be easy to see Dad with a new baby, but that I would always be their number-one girl. I remember the black smudges from her mascara on the sleeves of her dressing gown after she wiped her eyes. I promised her that she'd always be my number one and that I'd never ever so much as like Clementine."

I pull the towel from my hair and burrow my face in it, willing it to have the same scent as Mum's dressing gown. But it smells of foreign detergent and my apple shampoo. I have no problem recalling Mum's convulsive sobs while I hugged her so tight I almost couldn't breathe. Even then, I didn't cry.

After the twins were born, it became much harder for Mum to see the stars.

—30—

On Saturday morning, Dad isn't feeling well. He comes staggering down the stairs, while I'm eating breakfast. His face is a greyish-yellow.

Eddie runs over to hug his legs, shouting, "Daddy, Daddy!"

Dad ruffles his hair.

Clementine appears from the office in a purple leotard, saying, "Are you feeling better?" Then she sees him, and her tone changes. "Oh, Will. You need to get back to bed. I'll get Maya to bring you a lemon-ginger tea before I go to my yoga class."

A little after ten, I meet Sunitha and Kiera outside Botanic Gardens station. I'm wearing the shorts Clementine bought me. When I left, she was staring at the embroidered pockets, as if she had X-ray vision. But I didn't bring my Swiss Army knife, although I feel unprepared without it.

At the bottom of an extremely long escalator, Cheryl Yi's waiting for us, because she's come from another line. She's sitting on the floor. It's so squeaky clean you could eat off it, if there weren't signs everywhere with crossed-out food, stating fines of up to five hundred dollars for doing so.

The train's full and we have to stand.

"Gosh, this place is packed like anchovies. I can't believe you haven't been to Chinatown yet. We'll show you everything!" Kiera squeals. "It'll be sooo much fun! My mum has this route she always walks with our visitors. I've been on it like a million times."

"My grandparents used to live in Chinatown," Cheryl Yi says, but Kiera goes on, telling me about temples and chopstick shops and a wet market with fish. I don't ask, but I wonder if it's some kind of water tank where you can catch your own fish, which would be really cool.

Every time the train approaches a station, a voice says "Please mind the gap" and something like "Be happy happy". I listen for a couple of stations before I ask Cheryl Yi why they're telling us to be happy happy. She giggles and tells me they're saying, "*Berhati-hati di ruang platform*," which means "Mind the gap" in Malay.

Another escalator packed with people delivers us above ground in a futuristic glass station building. It's squeezed in between old shophouses in primary colours. Cheryl Yi leads us through the hordes, because Kiera can't remember the way.

In the market, it's mainly the floor that's wet, because it's being washed down with hoses. The stallholders wear wellies. They sell all kinds of fish—even a three-metre-long shark. In a corner, there's a stall with frogs and small turtles in cages. And it isn't a pet shop. While we're watching, the Chinese stallholder kills a frog with the blow of a mallet. Kiera and Sunitha gasp and hide behind their hands. Cheryl Yi shrugs.

I stare in fascination. But Sunitha is pulling us away and outside, saying, "Let's wait a while before we go to the hawker centre to eat."

"Come, Freja, you have to see this." Kiera drags me towards a monumental temple. Before we enter, Sunitha helps me tie a borrowed shawl around my bare legs. Inside, everything is red and orange and gold. Upstairs, one of Buddha's teeth is exhibited in a golden cage behind glass. On a raised platform, a man in a suit is sitting cross-legged, with closed eyes.

Kiera sighs. "Just imagine—in here, all that glitters really is gold!"

"Do you know where Pagoda Street is?" I ask Cheryl Yi.

"Of course. That's where we came out of the MRT."

The meditating man opens his eyes and shushes us.

"And Macao Street?" I whisper.

Cheryl Yi shrugs and shakes her head. I search the map on my phone, but the only Macao Streets I find are in China or even further away. Ling must've misremembered the street name, which makes me wonder if I can trust any of her memories.

As soon as we've taken off the scratchy shawls and are outside the temple, I ask about hungry ghosts. Cheryl Yi shows me an old oil drum where people are allowed to burn offerings.

"So, what exactly are they burning?" I ask her. Half-rotten pumpkin must be difficult to ignite. And there are shapes in the oil drum that are much bigger than the hell banknotes.

"Joss paper," she says. "Banknotes or paper effigies. There's a *kimzua* shop around the corner where my *ah ma* goes."

She leads us to a shop bursting with colour. Even Kiera goes quiet, while we look at everything from life-size dogs, toiletries and *Smsung* phones, to canned *Ice Tee* and *Caca Cola*, *McDnalds* fast-food and whole meals with desserts. Every item's made of paper or thin carton and meant to be burnt for the hungry ghosts.

"Why is everything spelt wrong?" Sunitha asks.

"The spelling mistakes are on purpose," Cheryl Yi explains, "because nothing in the underworld is supposed to be the same as here."

Kiera opens a pink cardboard laptop with a white apple logo and *McBook* written on the outside. "I wish I had a new computer instead of a hand-me-down," she says and strokes the paper keyboard.

I wonder what Ling might like. Perhaps a red school bag, with a matching pencil case and notebooks. It only costs four dollars.

"So how does it work?" Sunitha asks. "You burn these, and then what? Your ancestors can use them in the afterlife?"

"Or the smoke might appease wandering ghosts. You want them happy, so they don't hang around after the seventh month."

"Can they do that?" I ask.

"Unless the Hell Guards find them and bring them back."

"The Hell Guards?" Sunitha asks.

Cheryl Yi rolls her eyes. "You must've seen them, Kiera?"

"Mmm... There's a cow and a horse, right?" Kiera's holding cardboard computers in four colours, saying she wants to buy one to send a signal to her parents. I'm glad, because then it'll look less strange if I buy a gift for Ling.

"I have an idea," Cheryl Yi says. "We should go to Haw Par Villa to see the underworld and the Hell Guards. It's weird and haunted and only like five or six stops on the Circle Line."

While Kiera's paying, the shopkeeper hands me the paper school bag.

"Can we do some living-people shopping, first?" Sunitha starts talking about what she wants to buy, but I'm not listening.

Next to the counter is a stand with paper effigies I hadn't noticed earlier. A baby care set contains nappies, dummies, milk bottles and silent rattles. Paper playsets for little boys and girls are filled with cars and building blocks or dolls with extra clothes. Toys to keep babies and toddlers occupied in the afterlife. Dead babies and toddlers.

All the colours become a swirling blur.

—31—

Kiera and Sunitha drag me out of the shop and across a road with streaks of yellow and blue taxis. Although they're talking to me, all I hear is the buzzing noise of a thousand bees. They sit me down somewhere crowded, and then Cheryl Yi is by my side.

"Drink this!" She shoves a sweating plastic cup with a straw into my hand. Her voice is muffled.

I take a long slurp. Gradually, the colours around me settle into people and objects. I'm sitting on a plastic stool at a round plastic table. Next to Cheryl Yi, two Kleenex packets lie on the table above empty stools, but the other four places are occupied by strangers. Between quick chopstick movements, they're peeking at me. I have no idea where I am, and I'm unsure how I got here.

"Nice lemonade," I say after another sip.

"Lime juice. Same same, but different." Cheryl Yi's words are clear now, but she's almost drowned out by the noise of stools scraping against the floor and clattering trays and plates and chopsticks. There are people everywhere, talking and shouting. "The others are getting food. Will you be okay here for a short while? I'll be right back."

I nod and watch her make her way through the crowds along the endless row of food stalls. Unfamiliar smells waft towards me from sizzling frying pans and woks. Above the stalls, photos display the food they serve and prices between two and five dollars. I stare at the picture of a fish-head with milky eyes that's swimming in a bowl of soup with veggies, until Sunitha and Cheryl Yi return.

"I didn't like the look of the *dosa*, so I got *popiah* and *kueh pie tee* instead." Sunitha places a tray with plates of fresh spring rolls and tiny stuffed tart-shells on the table.

"I have *wanton mee* and carrot cake. It's not actually cake, Freja. More like an omelette," Cheryl Yi says. "You shouldn't eat Indian food in Chinatown anyway, Sunitha."

"I know," Sunitha says. "There wasn't a line. Speaking of lines... How far is Kiera?"

"She's next." Cheryl Yi points.

Kiera's standing by a triple-sized stall selling chicken rice. Behind her, in the queue that snakes around the corner, are at least fifty people. She arrives at the table with pale slices of chicken on fragrant rice, saying, "Good food comes to those who wait."

We share everything, and all the dishes are delicious. Sunitha even goes back to get more of the crispy one-bite tarts filled with salad and chopped shrimp.

After eating, I feel better. Perhaps it was just hunger and thirst and heat that made me dizzy. At least, that's what I tell the others.

"Now for the fun," Sunitha says, before we leave the hawker centre.

We browse in the front part of the small shops that sell bracelets and glittering hairbands and pencils and chopsticks and other bits and pieces, starting from one dollar. It's not my kind of fun! Shopping with Clementine would probably be better, because I'm sure she isn't so indecisive.

Kiera and Sunitha can't get enough. They go back and forth between shops, comparing prices. Cheryl Yi waits with me on a street corner. A horrible smell of rotten onion mixed with forgotten gym socks wafts around us. I wrinkle my nose and glance sideways at Cheryl Yi.

"Don't look at me. It's the durians," she says and points at a nearby stall which sells green spiky fruits the size of honeydew melons.

Behind the stall, I spot a street sign. *Pagoda Street* it says in English, with three Chinese symbols underneath. I survey the colourful houses on the narrow street, wondering where Ling used to live.

"D'you know where the slum is? Or was?"

"We can try in there," Cheryl Yi says and points at a museum called the Chinatown Heritage Centre. She tells me they show how people lived in the old days.

"They were definitely poor," she says a few minutes later. We're upstairs in the museum, studying a tiny room—as small as Maya's—where up to six people slept on short shelf-like bunks. The toilet is shared with the whole floor and part of the kitchen.

The "old days" turn out to be the 1950s, so not quite as far back as when I'm guessing Ling was here. At that time, my grandmother grew up on the farm where both she and Aunt Astrid and my uncle and cousins live now. I wonder how they would feel about being cramped in here with less space than egg-laying hens in battery cages. I wonder how much worse it was when Ling was alive.

"Isn't it funny," Cheryl Yi says, "most people don't realize this is here? They think we can just forget the past and rewrite our history. Everyone focuses on building the future."

When Sunitha texts to say they've spent their pocket money and are ready to go, I'm reading a sign about Pagoda Street. It used to be full of opium dens and slave traders and must have been the worst slum in the city.

Before we descend the escalator to the MRT, I glance back towards the financial district, trying to spot Dad's building. Skyscrapers and steel-and-glass office buildings rise up behind the old shophouses. On the surface, Singapore might look like a modern city, but it's as if there's a different world underneath the shiny varnish. A world populated by ghosts of the past.

Haw Par Villa is a bizarre collection of painted statues. Many of them are bigger than me. Some are huge. Most are arranged to illustrate Chinese myths about curious characters I've never heard of. It's like an outdoor Madame Tussauds, with mythical creatures instead of famous people.

"You've never heard of Monkey God?" Cheryl Yi asks, in a tone that I would use with someone who'd never heard the story of *The Little Mermaid*. "Sun Wukong. Also called the Monkey King?"

Both Sunitha and Kiera shake their heads with me.

"He's like the best hero ever. Incredibly strong and so fast that with one somersault he's on the other side of the globe." She drags us to a towering fake mountain, crawling with monkeys as big as us in colourful clothes. The crowned monkey reigns from the very top.

On the way to the exhibit of the underworld, we pass grotesque statues—like Pigsy, a man with a pig's head, and others of human heads attached to the bodies of spiders or turtles or crabs. Some are spooky, but not scary.

Tigers prowl on every corner, but none of them are white. I stop to stroke a blue-green dragon on the bump between its eyes. Although it doesn't look much like the real azure dragon, it makes me wonder if he has put out the fire, and how the other mythical creatures will ever get out of the pit if we don't help them.

We shouldn't have left that world in such a mess. At the thought, the cobwebs in my memory loft flutter.

"Wake up, Freja." Sunitha shakes my shoulder. "You're miles away."

I pat the dragon one last time, before I follow her to the Ten Courts of Hell. The Hell Guards, Ox-head and Horse-face, watch over the entrance. Their bodies are human and powerful, but one has the head of a bull, the other the head of a horse. They glare down at us. Ox-head frowns. Horse-face's nostrils flare, his teeth bared in a menacing sneer.

"They chase spirits into the realm of the dead with their spears and make sure they don't escape," Cheryl Yi says.

Sunitha shudders. "I'm glad I'm not a ghost."

"Someone should repaint them," Kiera says. "Then they might be a bit creepy." She picks at a flake of peeling paint on horse-face's cloak.

"Don't touch them!" I yell. The strange buzzing in my ears is back.

Kiera stares back at me with a raised eyebrow.

The others enter the realm of the dead, but I'm scared of going inside. I can't help fearing that somehow the Hell Guards will raise their spears and block the entrance, so I can't ever leave.

I'm also feeling dizzy again and take a swig of my water bottle.

Cheryl Yi pops back out. "What are you waiting for, Freja? Sunitha and Kiera are on their way out on the other side."

Holding my hands like blinkers, I slip past the two guards, in through the open gates.

Ahead, Sunitha says, "Ewww."

Kiera answers, "It's only red paint."

I hurry past the displays, hardly looking into the glass showcases where small figures are being decapitated, thrown into volcanos, having their hearts cut out or their intestines removed, or suffering other terrifying punishments.

Ling's only a child, and she hasn't committed any crimes, so she can't have been in a place like this. And I'll do everything to ensure she won't be returning to one.

—32—

"Tonight, of all nights. Why does your daddy have to be sick tonight?" Clementine's saying to Billy and Eddie, when I get home. "Can you come and take the boys, Maya?" she calls. She's standing by the dining table, her back turned to me.

Billy has grabbed a handful of her floor-length, glittering-gold dress.

Eddie holds a board book towards her, yelling, "Stor-ry, stor-ry."

"Maya!"

Maya's bare feet pitter-patter across the marble floor, before she unclenches Billy's fist and frees the dress.

"Frej-ja," Eddie says when he sees me.

Clementine turns. "There you are, Freja. Did you have a nice time?" Before I can answer, she's already turned back to the table and is trying to fit things from an oversized handbag into a small sparkly clutch.

"It was great," I say, walking past her to the stairs, holding the crinkled plastic bag from the paper-offering shop out of sight.

"I'd love to hear all about it, but my driver's here. It's so annoying your daddy has food poisoning. I was counting on his support." In her high-heeled sandals, she click-clacks out of the door and into the waiting limousine.

Upstairs, I sneak a peek into the master bedroom where Dad's sleeping. When I open my own door, Lizzie flitters across the floor. Ling's sitting on my bed.

"Did you find the house?" I ask and stuff the plastic bag into my wardrobe. I want to keep it as a surprise.

"I am not sure... I found a house that looked almost like it, on a street called Goodwood Hill. But everything is different from what I remember. Where there used to be rainforest, there are houses and they are so tall they reach the clouds."

While Ling is speaking, I've already turned on my laptop and searched for Goodwood Hill. On the satellite map, it's a green island in a sea of skyscrapers. I skim the first websites and read the important bits aloud.

"It says the black-and-whites on Goodwood Hill were some of the oldest... from 1903... built for civil servants of the British colonial administration and senior military personnel..." I turn to Ling. "Are doctors civil servants? Then it would fit with your dad being a doctor."

It's only now that I notice her staring at my laptop. I guess they didn't even have TV when she was alive.

"It's a computer. It's like... like a library of information. Do you know what a library is?" When she nods, I go on. "A library of all the information in the whole world.

164

Unfortunately, there isn't a real librarian, so it can be hard to find what you're looking for."

After I try searching for doctors in Singapore and get about a million hits, I slam the laptop lid down. Perhaps I should go to Goodwood Hill. I'd much rather be outside investigating, like Kalle Blomkvist, my favourite detective, than sitting in front of a computer screen. But it's too late and I'm too tired to go anywhere now.

"I was in Pagoda Street today." I show Ling photos on my phone of the colourful shophouses. "Recognize any of them?"

"It is all so different now..."

"But there isn't a... wait..." I flip through my notebook until I get to the page where I've jotted down details Ling has told me. "There isn't a Macao Street in Singapore. Are you sure that was the name?"

"Yes. I was there every day, asking for work. I remember the smells and the noise. Sawdust and stone dust filled the air. Sawing and hammering and chiselling could be heard from every shop. And weeping widows and daughters and mothers."

"I believe you," I hurry to say.

On my computer, I find out that Macao Street was renamed to Pickering Street, but no matter what I try, I can't find out when it happened. I sink back in my chair.

"Right now, an internet librarian would be helpful."

"I always wanted to go to the library," Ling says after a quiet pause. "William told me about the rows of bookshelves. Sir used to take him to Raffles Library on Saturday afternoons. Afterwards, I would sit with William on the steps of the veranda. He would make me read aloud from the books he had borrowed and help me learn new words. Sir would be in a chair under the fan, reading his newspaper. He was always reading the newspaper. Sometimes, I would sneak behind him and read over his shoulder about rubber prices and which ships were in the harbour. But after Sir remarried, my life changed."

"You don't remember seeing a date anywhere on a newspaper, do you?"

After a moment, she shakes her head.

"Wait a minute... My class went to the Royal Danish Library and saw these ancient machines where you used to read microfilm of old newspapers. Now, they're all on computers. Perhaps it's the same here! Let's see."

A moment later, I'm on the website for the National Library Board of Singapore. They have local newspapers from the last two hundred years available online. It takes me less than five minutes to find what we need.

"You're a genius, Ling! Look! This is brilliant. Here's an article where it says that Macao Street will be renamed to Pickering Street on 1. January 1925. So now we are much closer to knowing when you died. It must've been between 1922 when the cemetery opened and 1925 when the street was renamed. The puzzle pieces are falling into place. We're master detectives!" I hold my right hand up for a high-five, but of course Ling doesn't know what to do, and my hand would pass right through hers anyway.

"I think... perhaps... Sir was called William too," Ling says hesitantly. "Ma cried out for him that evening."

I immediately try searching the 1920s newspapers for someone named William Brimsten, like Dad, but I get no results, and searching for William gives me thousands of hits. "Was everyone called William back then?" I mutter.

Then I notice that Ling has slid down and is kneeling on the floor.

"I remember that evening... We were sitting like this on the lawn—William, my brother, and I—with one of the big library books. The sweet scent of the night flowers was heavy in the air. It was dark, but we had a lantern..."

Ling's voice is low and husky. Her eyes are open, but it's almost like she's in a trance. Reacting quickly, I switch off the lights, and sit down on the floor across from her, placing my opened biology book between us. I turn my torch on at the dimmest setting and hold it over the text.

"Ma'am—William's stepmother—came out on the veranda and watched us. I thought she would berate William for spending time with a servant and teaching me to read, like she always did. Instead, she started screeching and ran into the house. She hauled Ma from the kitchen to the street by Ma's hair, which she had twisted out of its bun. Ma wept while Ma'am screamed English words I had never heard before. She wanted to throw me out too, but Cook complained and said she needed her kitchen maid.

"I did not understand what had happened until later that night. When the house was dark and Cook was snoring, William found me and led me to the looking glass in the hallway. He kneeled so our heads were next to each other, then he held a candle between us and the mirror and told me to look. The flame threw our faces into colourless contours of light and darkness. Identical shadows of square chins showed on our necks. Four eyebrows with the exact same shape rose in surprise. Dimples made black holes on both our cheeks. Our twin reflections smiled. William embraced me and called me his beloved sister..."

"Beloved sister," I repeat in a whisper. The words bounce around inside me, like an echo.

"The next day, hidden by the banana trees, Ma told me the truth. She said she had always loved William, and at that moment she didn't mean my brother."

"What did your father do?"

"Nothing. I do not think anyone told him. He was seriously ill. I remember that now. That was the reason they sailed for England. When they left, William promised to come back. But he forgot his promise. He forgot he had a beloved sister."

—33—

On Sunday morning, I stay in bed with my laptop, and skim through newspaper articles and notices from a hundred years ago about people called William. Hearing Ling's story has made me more determined than ever to discover how we're related. If we're related. I'm not sure I'd be proud of having Ling's brother as my ancestor. After all his promises, he just left her to die.

I exit my room with perfect timing; as I close my door, Dad comes upstairs with a twin under each arm.

"Hello sleepy-head," he says. He still looks like he ought to be in bed. "These two are ready for a nap and so am I. We've been up since six, haven't we, boys? And Mummy says we've watched too much telly."

"Tel-ly," Eddie says, drooling on the floor. Billy giggles and wiggles against Dad's hold.

"Stay here, Billy!"

It's stupid that I've never thought about it, but I suddenly realize that Billy is short for William. "Granddad's first name was also William, right?" I ask. "What about his father?"

"His father..." Dad pushes the door to the twins' room open with his foot, "...was called Robert and my grandma was called Mina." He drops Billy in his cot, before he deposits Eddie on the changing table.

I stay by the open door. "And Robert's father?"

"Frej-ja, Frej-ja," Billy chants until it's his turn. While Dad is changing his nappy, Billy struggles.

"I don't remember. Are you doing a genealogy chart for scho—"

Billy kicks the container of baby powder Dad's holding. It flies across the room and lands in a puff of white. A snow-like sprinkle settles on the wooden floor.

"Just what I needed." Dad sighs.

"I can help, Dad. D'you need me to get the hoover?"

"I'll wipe it up. But if you could read them their story, that'd be great."

"Let me do the cleaning," I say, but Dad's already on his knees with a bunch of wet wipes.

"Stor-ry!" Eddie waves with a picture book.

"You're staying here, right?" I ask, and Dad nods, before I make my way around him and the white dust to the beanbag in the corner, between the two cots.

While I'm reading the story for the second time, even Billy quiets down and stops shoving toys through the bars. Eddie falls asleep, clutching the neck-hem of my T-shirt, his warm breath on my arm. I feel myself relaxing.

When I glance up after finishing the book, Dad's watching me and smiling. He picks up a soft doggy and tucks it under

Billy's arm. I gently unfold Eddie's fingers, before we tiptoe out of the room.

On his way into the master bedroom, Dad yawns. I skip downstairs. He's given me an idea.

Clementine sits at the dining table. Her laptop's open, showing a photo collage of men with bow ties and women in long, shimmering dresses.

"The event was perfect," she says, although I haven't asked. "We almost doubled the amount of money from last year. In the end, it didn't matter that Will couldn't make it." She chats on about the perfect crayfish starter, the brilliant band and the full dance floor, as if I'm one of her girlfriends. As if she's forgotten how she screamed at me two days ago.

While the twins are taking their nap, I go out to the pool. I draw a family tree in my notebook. After some mulling, I add the years I know, like when Dad and I were born. If Ling was twelve when she died between 1922 and 1925, and her brother was almost four years older, then he must've been born between 1906 and 1909. I fill the gap between him and Dad with ancestors. I'm not that good at maths, but the drawing helps. Ling's brother could actually have been my great-great-grandfather.

After I cross out the Danish branches on my tree, there are only four possible great-great-grandfathers left. It shouldn't be difficult to find out their names.

I call the one person who might be able to help: Granny. No answer. A few minutes later, though, she sends me a message that she's on the way to a conference in Istanbul and will call back when she has Wi-Fi and time.

In the shade by the pool, I continue to search for Ling's brother or father in the newspaper archive. When squeals jerk me out of a snooze, my laptop's sticking to my thighs and the screen has gone black. Above, fluffy dark-grey clouds roll across the sunless sky. On the lounger next to mine, Clementine taps away on her phone. The twins are running around the pool in bulky, long-sleeved swimsuits. The blue-clad twin hits the one in green with a ball. The green twin, Eddie, wails.

"Stop that, Billy," Clementine says, without looking up from her phone.

Eddie crouches and lowers a toy watering can into the pool. He wobbles as he pulls it out of the water. I sit up. From under the palm tree by the hedge, Ling waves at me. I hadn't realized it was so late.

"Can they swim?" I ask. Of all survival skills, being able to swim is definitely the most important. "Shouldn't they wear arm bands?" It comes out woolly because my mouth is fuzzy after sleeping outside.

"Their suits are inflated," Clementine says. "And we're right here."

Billy's now on a scooter, rolling along the tiles around the pool, too close to the water. Eddie's watering the lawn.

Clementine asks if I want something to drink. I'm thirsty, but Dad isn't here, and I don't want Clementine to leave me alone with them.

Unfortunately, Billy has heard her. "Drink, Mummy," he yells.

Clementine puts her phone in the pocket of her sundress. "I'll bring coconut water for all of you."

"I can get it," I hurry to say.

"Relax, Freja."

But how can I relax when I'm alone with them? I scoot forward to sit at the edge of the lounger.

A phone's ringing inside the house. Clementine answers. Eddie returns with his watering can. Billy drives faster and faster on his scooter.

"Clementine!" I call. "Dad!" I stand up and glance back over my shoulder into the house.

There's a splash. I turn. Billy's giggling. He's on the scooter by the water's edge, right where Eddie was a moment ago. Then Eddie resurfaces with a loud cry.

"Help!" I scream. I can't move.

Eddie's chubby little arms whisk the water. He's wailing.

Clementine comes running. On her knees, she reaches into the water and fishes Eddie out. Snot bubbles out of his nose, onto her drenched dress. She gazes at me and frowns.

After Clementine has taken the twins inside, Ling floats across the pool. "Why did you not jump in the water and help him?" she asks. "You are good at swimming."

"I don't know." I slump down on the sun lounger and squeeze my hands under my thighs to stop them from shaking. "It's just... What if I'd jumped in and landed on Eddie, so he couldn't breathe? And then he would've died, and everyone would be unhappy." I take a ragged breath. "And it would be my fault."

Suddenly cold, I wrap the towel around my shoulders.

Ling turns and studies the pool. "I doubt you could jump so far," she says.

173

But that's not the part I want her to convince me is unrealistic.

When I sneak into the house, the twins are watching their bilingual programme and don't notice me. I've almost reached the top of the stairs before I hear Clementine's raised voice from the office.

"We have to do something about her, Will. I'm worried about the twins. She needs professional help. You can't pretend it never happened. Look at Marianne—"

Afraid to overhear any more, I run into my bathroom and turn on the shower. It blocks out all sounds, but not the image of silky cobweb-threads snapping.

—34—

It's Tuesday evening before Granny calls back.

I've spent the afternoon at Kiera's, giggling at jokes and her big brothers' banter. All three are on the school's basketball teams and made the lounge appear small. When two of them—Liam and Cillian—got into a scuffle over the last muffin, the whole house shook with slamming doors and rattling windows.

"My life—living with three elephants in the room," Kiera said as she walked me home to get away from the "doggy dog world" at her house. While she moaned about her brothers, I kept thinking how much nicer it would be to have older siblings.

"Will you stop complaining!" I finally said, surprising her so much she was quiet for several seconds.

Now, it's after dinner. Ling's sitting in my window seat with her head leaning against her knees. And I'm sitting on my bed in the same position. We've hit a wall. Ling can't find the exact house—perhaps it isn't there any more—and

I can't find the right William anywhere on the internet. Time's running out. In four days, the Hungry Ghost Festival is over. Ling's holiday will end.

"*Darling,*" Granny shouts, when I answer the video call. "*It's lovely to see you.*"

She's holding her phone so I can see her chin from below, her red lipstick and right up her nostrils.

"*How's Singapore? I always find it terribly humid. I shall come for a quick visit next month, anyway—did your father tell you? Are you having a wonderful time with the little rascals? Aren't they adorable?*"

I'm nodding away, relieved there's no need for me to answer any of Granny's questions.

"*Have you started school? Are you making—*"

"Yes. Last week. I'm doing this family tree and I thought you might help with the names of my great-great-grandparents."

After she has listed her own parents and grandparents—no Williams among them—and told me several anecdotes about them, I interrupt her again.

"And Granddad's? His parents were called Robert and Mina, right?"

"*Let me see… Your great-grandfather's parents were Mary and William, and Mina's parents were William Henry and Lily. Everyone was named William or John or Thomas back then.*"

Two Williams. "And their surnames?"

"*Obviously, Robert's parents were Brimstens, like we are, and Mina's…*" Granny's leaning her forehead against the phone while she's thinking, then gives me a sweeping view of her hotel room's ceiling as she zooms out again. "*For the life of me, I can't remember Wilhelmina's maiden name. I only met her parents a couple of times. They lived overseas... The West Indies, I believe."*

"Can you find out, please? It's important."

"Do you have to hand it in this week?"

I nod and don't feel bad about pretending this is a school assignment. I need to know by Saturday.

"Tell you what... I'm flying back to London tomorrow afternoon... There's a box of old photos and papers from Mina in the cellar. It's been there for years, but I haven't really looked at it... I'm certain there are documents with her maiden name. And your father can even bring photos for your chart and whatever else I find—he's coming round Friday before his late flight back to Singapore."

Granny ends the call by kissing her screen, giving me a close-up of her nose before it turns to orange blur.

An hour ago, when Dad left for the airport, I was cross he wouldn't return until Saturday afternoon. Now, it might actually be helpful that he's going to London. Crazy, though. Who travels to the other side of the world for a three-day meeting?

"Is she gone?" Ling floats around me, studying my phone from all angles, as if Granny would somehow be hiding behind it. "I wish I had seen my grandparents." She sighs. "But Ma's parents lived in China... Sometimes, after we had been to the temple, Ma would go to the letter-writer so she could send them news and money. She never told them the truth about me. I think she was scared of my grandmother."

"Mum's a bit scared of Granny. Once, she put off calling her for a whole day—she was so nervous."

"Why? Your grandmother is nice."

177

Why was that? I'm trying to remember. "Mum was walking around the house saying, 'Your grandmother's not going to believe it. She's going to insist you come to the wedding'."

"Which wedding?" Ling asks.

"Dad and Clementine's. Oh, I remember now. I was supposed to be a flower girl. The first time I met her, Clementine took my measurements for the flower-girl dress. The whole time, I was so afraid she would stumble on the measuring tape and land on her belly with the babies inside." I curl up on the bed, hugging my stomach. The flow of memories is coming so fast I can't stop them.

"The little boys?" Ling asks.

I nod. "In the week before the wedding, I had nightmares where Clementine slipped on the rose petals I'd scattered and everyone started crying. When I said I didn't want to go, Mum said I was being silly. But I stopped eating and said my tummy was aching. I was supposed to stay with Granny, that's why Mum had to call her. As soon as Mum had talked to Granny and Dad, my stomach ache disappeared.

"The day of the wedding, we were lying on the sofa, watching films. Mum asked if I wasn't a bit sad not to be a flower girl at a wedding with two hundred guests. And I almost thought she didn't know me at all until she winked. And then we were giggling and throwing pillows at each other. It's one of the best days I can remember."

Was that the last time the two of us had fun?

"But I can't ever tell that to Granny or Dad or Clementine. I promised Mum, Scout's honour. And now that I know Clementine, I'm sure she was probably upset about not having a flower girl."

"What is Scout's honour?"

"That's something you say when you make a promise if you're a girl guide or a scout... Was William a scout?"

Ling shakes her head.

"But he taught you Morse code?"

She smiles so widely, the dimples in her cheeks show up. "The secret 'dot-dash language', we used to call it."

I'm about to ask how William learnt it, if he wasn't a scout, when Ling goes on speaking:

"After Sir married the widow of his friend, William was not allowed to play or read with me. So we left messages for each other in our hiding places. Violet, Ma'am's daughter, could not understand our code, but she searched for our messages and tore the ones she found to pieces."

I'm remembering things, like the wedding day, I'd completely forgotten. And Ling's memories are more specific, with fewer missing details. Can it be because the fire's dying in the mythical world? Is the red colour in the north-west disappearing, and are these changes in *feng shui* impacting me as much as Ling?

Worst of all, what will happen to the hidden memory box once the red flames have been extinguished?

"Violet," I say, to think about something else. "That's one more name we can search for." I open my laptop but get too many results. Violet appears to have been another popular name. "Never mind. Granny will find William's surname tomorrow."

I don't tell Ling that if she doesn't, then I have no clue what to try next.

—35—

After school on Wednesday, I slide into the empty seat next to Jason on the school bus. It's always the last seat to get taken. I'm not sure if it's because he takes up more than half of the double seat, or because he's so unfriendly. I've still hardly talked to him since our so-called play date. But I know from Kiera that he's in her Mandarin class, and this morning I had an idea.

As usual, the cord from Jason's earphones hangs from his ears, and he's staring out the window. He doesn't react when I say his name, so I tap him on the shoulder.

He turns with a wide-eyed scared expression, then frowns.

"Don't do that," he hisses, before he leans back against the window, ignoring me. Even for him, that's rude.

The bus is too small to move around in, so I stay, sitting stiffly, on the very edge of the seat, pushing my own music into my ears. I tell myself it doesn't matter, that perhaps I can get Kiera to help, even though it will mean lots of long explanations. Today would be perfect though—for once it isn't raining.

Jason follows me off the school bus.

"You shouldn't tap people on their shoulders during the seventh month. That's what ghosts do," he says. "What did you want?"

"Never mind." I yank my earphones out. "If you weren't so rude, I would've asked for your help. But you're probably too scared to help me, anyway." I rummage through the front pocket of my school bag for my key.

"Too scared to do what?"

"To come with me to Bukit Brown and help me decipher an inscription."

"What? Now?" He turns paler and bites his lip. "I'm not *pantang*," he mutters to himself.

I look him up and down. Like me, he's wearing the school uniform shorts. "You need to change into trousers and a long-sleeved top. I'll meet you outside your house in an hour." Before he can find an excuse, I'm through the gate and inside our house.

I gobble Maya's snacks and tell Clementine I'm going over to Jason's. She's "so happy" we've become friends. I even wave at her and the twins when I leave by the front door. Then I double back and retrieve my combat trousers, hiking boots and the other stuff I've hidden in the tree below my window. I've already tugged my climbing rope down.

As we're hiking up the road, I tell Jason about Ling. The air is buzzing. He doesn't even blink when I show him photos of her Morse messages, and he's impressed with the information we've found online. Kiera would've taken more convincing.

When I tell him about how Ling led me to the enormous banyan tree, he says, "You really shouldn't follow ghosts," in a voice that makes me shudder despite the heat. I decide not to tell him anything about what happened inside the banyan tree. Even he wouldn't believe that.

Jason's wearing jeans, so he can't have much in terms of survival equipment on him. My Swiss Army knife is back in my pocket; without it and my other gear, I'd feel unprepared. Before we leave the trail, I lend him my mosquito spray. He spritzes it onto his hands and neck, while I find him a suitable stick.

"Snake protection," I say when I hand it to him.

His eyes widen, then he pulls a keyring with at least ten keys out of his pocket and shakes them. "Ghost protection," he says. He jangles the keys noisily, all the way to Ling's grave—even while I hold the prickly bushes aside and help him into the little grove.

A scatter of pebbles from Ling's last message are still on the flat gravestone. The sticks must have gone with the rain or been carried off by ants.

"I wanted you to see the Chinese signs." I lead him to the other side of the upright stone.

It's a wild shot. The other sign on Ling's gravestone is more crumbled-away than I remembered, and it's unlikely that she was buried with William's surname. Still... After talking to Granny last night, it seemed possible that we could solve the mystery in time. But even if Granny finds Mina's maiden name, that still doesn't prove that Mina's father and Ling's brother are the same person. It isn't proof we're related.

While I jangle the keys for him, Jason borrows my torch and studies the signs, tracing the etching with his fingers.

"You're right, this one means 'Ling'. But this one... Can I borrow your pencil and some paper?"

In my notebook, he draws a sign that resembles two three-legged dancers.

林

"It's only this part that's still visible," he says, circling the bottom-right quarter. "So it could be another sign."

"Wow! How did you know?"

"Because it means 'Lim' or 'Lin'. It's my family name, too, and quite common. Keep jangling the keys or give them to me."

The leaves rustle near the place we entered the grove.

"Can we get out of here?" Jason snatches the keys from me and backs away from the sound, while he jangles them wildly. "Now!"

"Let's go this way. It might be a snake." I stride away, in the direction of the asphalt pathway with the pauper's section sign, banging my stick with every step. Jason puffs and jangles keys behind me until I hear a yelp and a dull thump.

He's stumbled over the hidden remains of a statue—one of the small lions that are everywhere in the graveyard.

"Why're the lions playing ball?" I ask, as I help him up. The lion statues have either a ball or an even smaller lion between their front paws.

"Ball?" He snickers. "It's not a ball. It's the earth. Male lions have the world at their feet, females have baby lions.

Don't you know anything?" After taking in my expression, he stops grinning. "Sorry."

We walk on, to the sound of sticks and keys, and twigs snapping beneath our feet.

"Freja, I've been thinking," Jason pants. I wait for him to catch up. "Hungry ghosts can be tricksters. They'll do bad things to get revenge over those who hurt them."

"Ling isn't like that."

"Maybe not, but are you absolutely sure she's telling the truth?"

"There's no way she could've faked those memories. I was there. I saw how they affected her."

"But isn't it odd she only remembered everything now?"

I shake my head. I can't tell him about the dragon who's putting out the fire in the north-west. He would want proof. And I don't want to go back to that world ever again.

When he spots the pathway, Jason jogs onto the cracked asphalt. Here, he exhales, as if he has reached a safe harbour.

"Even if her story's true," he says, "you still might not be related. I mean, this place is full of wandering spirits. Perhaps she latched onto your dad because he's called William and has yellow hair and blue eyes."

I'm quiet while we walk towards the cemetery exit. I don't want to believe Jason, but the thousands of Williams in the old newspapers make me uncertain. Ling has always been so focused on our hair and eye colours. What else links us to her memories?

"The enormous banyan tree is up there." I point at the natural tunnel through the elephant-ear-like leaves. It's right behind a massive grave with golden inscriptions on the shining reddish marble. Although I don't want to go inside the root cage, I'm tempted to show him the tree.

"*Aiyoh!* Look at the state of this food." Jason steps around the blackened, burnt paper on the ground in front of the grave. A whole meal with rice and soya sauce has been served for the ancestor. Now, a highway of ants covers the plate like a black undulating carpet draped over the food.

"Is that really what your ghosts want? I know some restaurants serve ants, and I guess I'd eat them in a survival situation, but this is disgusting."

"I told you already, what they want is to be honoured and remembered."

"And now that I know Ling's story, I can remember her. Isn't that enough? And I can see her. That must be proof we're related."

"Not necessarily..." Jason pushes his fringe back and squints at me sideways. "You could be a medium. Have you seen any other ghosts?" The gate's in sight, and he stuffs the keys back in his jeans pocket.

"No, I haven't, and I've been spending a lot of time in this graveyard."

"Well, if I was a ghost and had one month's holiday from a horrible place, I wouldn't hang around in an old graveyard. I'd go out and have fun."

I roll my eyes. "Like in a theme park? You'd go to Sentosa?"

"Nope. I'd go to a *getai*."

Before I can ask what he's talking about, Ling floats out from behind a normal-sized banyan tree, saying, "Can I come too? I love *getai*."

"Hi Ling," I say.

"What? Is she here?" The keys are out again, and Jason's jangling them furiously.

I nod. "She's standing right in front of you. Can you stop that noise?"

Ling's holding her hands over her ears. I want to do the same. When he puts the keys away, with a sheepish look, I go on. "This is Jason, Ling. He's helping us."

Ling waves at Jason, who obviously can't see her, because he's gazing in a slightly different direction.

"What's a *getai*?" I ask.

They both start speaking at the same time. Ling's whole face lights up. From what I can understand, it's some kind of show.

"*Ah Ma*'s helping at one tonight," Jason says. He checks his watch. "It begins at half-past seven. We can take a bus from Lornie Road."

I ought to let Clementine know where I'm going, but what

if she wants me to come home? I've told her I'm at Jason's, so she won't worry, I think, before I turn off my phone.

On the way to the *getai*, I sit behind Jason. I hope the bus won't be so full someone will want the apparently empty seat next to me, where Ling is floating. She says she has to concentrate to avoid gliding backwards through the seat or landing next to Jason whenever the driver hits the brakes.

I lean forward. "Where are your parents?" I ask so quietly Jason can ignore my question. If he's an orphan, he might not want to talk about it, and Dad says my Danish bluntness can be more of a curse than a blessing.

"Somewhere in the Indian Ocean," he answers.

For a moment I fear I was right, that they're dead. Drowned.

Then he swings round to face me and says, "They're marine biologists. They met when Dad studied in Germany— my mum's German—and they've wanted to save the oceans ever since. That's why I live with *Ah Ma*. During the school holidays, I usually get to fly out to wherever they are and stay on the boat. This summer they picked me up in Tasmania. It was fantastic, but freezing cold."

I'm speechless. It sounds like it's actually fine for him not to live with his parents—both of them—for months. "Do you talk to them every day?"

"Nah. Depends where they are. At the moment, once a week over their satellite phone. But I hear their voices every day. They're doing this podcast, called *Post from a Plastic Ocean* every Wednesday. I always listen to it on the school bus."

So that's what he was listening to when I thought he was being rude. "And it's okay, living with your grandmother?"

"It's great. Mostly, it's great. She worries a lot more than my parents. And she treats me like I'm still five years old. And she buys me the ugliest T-shirts, which I only wear inside the house. But she's doing her best."

I nod. I know what it's like to be treated like a five-year-old.

We get off amid a cluster of identical high-rise blocks of flats with two-storey-high numbers on their sides. Long metal bars, with laundry hanging on them, stick out of some of the windows, like lonely hairs on a bald man's head. Jason leads the way between the buildings and through the grounds of a temple. An old man is lighting candles around its perimeter. He glances up when Ling passes close to him. Behind the temple, a party tent has been erected, and people—mostly elderly Chinese—stream in through the opening.

Inside, row after row of plastic chairs are lined up in front of a stage, and they fill up fast. It's so full, we can't find Jason's grandmother.

"Come on." Jason pushes me forward through the bustle. "Look!" He points at the first row of chairs, right in front of the stage. "What d'you see?"

"Er..." The front row must be reserved for VIPs, because it's empty, despite the fact that the seats on the many rows behind are fully occupied.

A man with a bowler hat and a glittering jacket enters the stage. A woman wearing a draped yellow dress and a matching, outlandish hat follows him. They start speaking into their microphones in rapid Chinese, constantly interrupting each other. Whatever they're saying must be funny, because many of the aunties and uncles laugh and clap.

"Look closely," Jason says, when the crowd quiets down. "Can you see anyone there?"

"Only Ling," I say. She's sitting alone in the very best seat, right in the middle of the empty front row. "What's she doing up there? Aren't those seats reserved?"

"Yep! They're reserved for the hungry ghosts."

"Twenty seats for ghosts or something happens," an auntie next to me says. "*Last time*, forget one chair and middle of performance something off the lights. Another time, some *ang mo* sit in front row and loudspeaker fall down."

A dancing troop with a sparkling singer have taken over the stage. The deafening sound makes the loudspeakers crackle. All the aunties sing along.

Jason starts pulling me towards the exit, shouting in my ear, "If you can't see any ghosts, then I doubt you're a medium."

"Wait. What about Ling?" I make my way to the side of the front row and try to catch her attention. She's busy clapping and singing. When she finally sees me, she waves me away. It looks like she doesn't want to give up her seat.

The pulse in my head pounds. The music is giving me a headache. My ears are still ringing when we're outside the tent.

"There's one more place we can try," Jason says, and he leads me to the MRT station instead of the bus. "The ghost station."

We stand on one of the long escalators down to the underground trains, while he explains.

"It's underneath Bukit Brown Cemetery. Above ground, you can only see the ventilation, but below, the platforms are ready for when the rainforest has been chopped down and replaced by housing."

As the train whooshes past a space that's slightly less dark than the rest of the tunnel, he shouts, "There! Did you see any ghosts?"

I shake my head.

We don't talk on the short walk home from Botanic Gardens station.

"Maybe it wasn't a good *getai*," Jason says outside our gate. "Maybe the ghosts couldn't be bothered turning up."

"Ling was having fun."

We've both stopped believing that I might be a medium. And I'm not sure if it should make me happy—because that means I really have a family connection with Ling—or sad because we're no closer to finding out how we're related. I still haven't heard from Granny.

Before going into the house, I turn on my phone, hoping Granny's left me a message. She hasn't. But my phone pings and pings with missed calls and texts from both Clementine and Dad, so I know I'm in trouble.

—37—

The texts are all variations of *Where are you?*, so I send Clementine an *I'm home* message, before I untie my hiking boots. She doesn't answer.

It's almost nine o'clock. I don't even try to go through the garden and my window but leave my boots outside the front door and open it warily, expecting a screeched telling-off like the other day. Instead, the house is deadly quiet.

"Hello," I call. The only answer is the hum of the air con. I head to the kitchen, but even Maya's gone.

The lounge seems huge, without anyone home. Like black mirrors, the windows take turns reflecting me, as I pace the room. At creaks from the gate, I feel both relief and dread.

Maya enters first, with the twins. She's jostling the double pushchair with the sleeping boys into the lounge. While she carries Billy upstairs, she sends me a small smile. Seconds later, after she's returned for Eddie, Clementine opens the front door.

She's not wearing a happy lipstick smile, but hiking boots, trekking pants and a long-sleeved top.

"Sorry," I hurry to say. "I turned my phone off to save battery. I'm sorry."

She doesn't say anything while she takes off her boots, then strides past me through the swing door to the kitchen. When she emerges a moment later, she sinks down on a dining chair and places her half-full glass of water directly on the table, breaking her own placemat or coaster rule.

"Where were you?" she says quietly, swirling the water glass. Behind her, Maya tiptoes into the kitchen.

"With Jason. We—"

"Do you know where Maya and the twins have been?" she asks, not even glancing at me.

I shrug.

"Out searching for you. Do you know where I have been?"

"Out searching for me," I say in the smallest possible voice, staring at the vortex in her glass, wishing it could carry me far away.

"Yes. In Bukit Brown Cemetery."

A twig is stuck in her hair, which hangs limply over her sweaty top.

"And do you know why?" Her eyes catch mine. "Because that was the last location of your phone."

I flinch at the sight of her glare. "You're spying on me?"

"Yes. I am. After I went over to Auntie Lim's to get her recipe for salted egg-yolk moon cakes and found the house empty. And after I tried both calling and texting you without any answer. And after I got Will out of an important meeting in London to ask if he knew where you were. Then, yes, I did check the location of your phone."

She's still speaking slowly in a normal tone, and it's much worse than if she was screeching.

"And your phone was in the one place I told you not to go... That cemetery isn't a playground. You could fall down somewhere. Break your leg. And how would we find you if your phone's turned off?"

She doesn't talk to me like I'm five years old, now, but she treats me like I am. Doesn't she understand that if I can survive in the Swedish wilderness, I'll be fine in a small patch of Singapore nature? I'm always careful when I go to the graveyard.

"I said I'm sorry." What does she want me to do? Fall on my knees? Why does she make such a big deal out of me being a bit late? Mum wouldn't worry after a couple of hours.

A tiny voice in my head whispers: *she might not even have noticed you were gone.*

But Clementine isn't Mum. She isn't *my* mum.

Everything that's wrong is *her* fault. Mum was almost fine until She married Dad. Dad was fine until She got him so obsessed with work and money. She probably forced him to accept the job in Singapore, just to take him far away from me.

"So, tell me again—where were you? And no lies."

"I'm. Not. Lying!" The surge of anger makes it difficult to speak. My voice shakes. "You told me not to go to the cemetery alone, and I didn't. I was with Jason. Afterwards, we went to a *getai*. I forgot to message you. So. What?"

"And you turned your phone off. Since you don't use it anyway, you can give it to me." She's standing now, holding a hand out until I place the phone in her palm. "And I'm sure you took that knife of yours. Hand it over! Don't think I won't search your pockets, young lady."

I pull my Swiss Army knife out and drop it on the dining table.

Her eyes are flashing. "I'm keeping these. And until Will gets back, you will stay in this house when you're not in school. You have to understand, when Will isn't here, I'm responsible for you."

"You're not my mother!" I yell right into her face.

"I know," she says.

And I wish it was Mum in front of me, so I could apologize and get a big hug. I can feel pressure behind my eyes. Like they're one of those canal dams I saw in Sweden. But I won't cry. Crying is useless. Instead, the pent-up water starts boiling.

"I wish I'd never come!" I scream.

"So do I!"

I turn and run up the stairs, yelling, "I'm glad I never came to your rotten wedding!"

"Wait, Freja. I didn't mean that," she calls, pursuing me upstairs.

I slam my door and lock it from the inside.

"Freja, please." She's banging on the door. "I didn't mean that. I was just so worried. I'm sorry, I snapped."

One twin begins crying, and then the other.

"Please open the door. I shouldn't have said that. I'm glad you're here."

I put my earphones in, but without the phone to play music, they don't mute the sound.

My pillow does. The knocking will stop soon. She'll go to the twins and calm them down. They're her children.

I can't help remembering what I overheard the other day. She's worried about Billy and Eddie, because I'm here. I don't belong in her happy family.

—38—

Clementine returned to knock on my door after the twins were quiet.

Deep down, I knew she wouldn't have called Dad unless she was extremely worried, so, in the end, I unlocked the door. While I stood in the half-open doorway, holding the handle and the door frame, we both said we were sorry. We didn't hug. She didn't give me my things back or un-ground me. I didn't tell her I have a way of leaving the house without her permission.

Ling was here during the night. I vaguely recall her telling me about the *getai*, and how she'd had to share her seat because the front row was packed with ghosts.

In the morning, I stay in my room until five minutes before the school bus stops outside our gate. Clementine isn't downstairs, but she knocked on my door earlier and offered to drive me to school so we could talk.

"What's wrong, Freja?" Sunitha asks during lunch break. "You haven't said a word all morning. And you keep slamming your books down and grinding your teeth."

"Yeah, it looks like you only keep your hair on because it's tied back," Kiera jokes.

"My stepmum's grounded me and taken my Swiss Army knife. And my phone."

"What? Why?" Cheryl Yi asks.

Kiera puts her half-eaten *roti prata* down. "Does that mean you can't come to my pyjama party tomorrow? Oh, you have to talk to her. I'll get my mum to call her."

I'd forgotten about the sleepover, and I'm suddenly glad I'm grounded. Tomorrow night might be my last night with Ling. "Please don't. That would make things worse."

"I didn't take her for a wicked stepmother." Sunitha slurps the rest of her lime juice.

"Me neither," Kiera says. "How can someone sooo pretty be sooo evil?"

"She isn't evil..." I think about Ling's memory of a real wicked stepmother. Clementine isn't like that. "I just don't want her to act as if she's my mum."

"But why did she ground you and confiscate your things?" Cheryl Yi asks again, pointing at me with the skewer from her *satay*. "What did you do?"

I try to explain that Jason was helping me find out how someone who's buried at Bukit Brown is related to me. Obviously, without mentioning that that someone has become my best friend.

Cheryl Yi says I'm crazy for running around a cemetery during the Hungry Ghost Festival. Sunitha wants to know if I like Jason and whether he talks more outside school. Kiera's mainly annoyed I'll miss her sleepover and can't even chat with them on my phone. And they're all shocked that I've been carrying a knife around Singapore.

When I tell Jason I've been grounded, he's relieved there won't be any more trips to the graveyard.

"I'm never going back to that place," he says, as the school bus rumbles down the hill. "Two nights, then the ghosts are gone and we have almost a year to find out who Ling's brother was. Next time my parents are in Singapore, my dad can help us search in the national archives." He holds one of his earphones out to me. "You wanna listen?"

The rest of the way home, I sit next to Jason while his parents are talking into my ear about marine conservation and single-use plastic, from somewhere freezing cold.

With Maya's afternoon snacks untouched on my desk, I read through my notebook, hoping to find something I've overlooked. I can't let Ling return to the underworld for another year.

When I open my laptop, there's a message from Granny. She writes that her flight was delayed, so she wasn't home until after midnight, and she won't have time to go through the box until after lunch.

Outside, it's still sunny and too early for Ling to come round. Lizzie clings to the window in front of me. Her tail curls into a spiral. With the light shining through her, I can see the veins in her body and the scales on her rubbery skin. She vibrates with every beat of her tiny heart. The transparency makes her look ghostly. It's enough of a reminder to keep searching.

I scroll through old newspapers on the library website. Some of the articles are useless but interesting, like the one about the man in Cardiff who amputated another man's arm with a penknife after an accident. When Ling arrives, I still haven't found anything helpful.

"In the last hour, I've skimmed though a month of birth, marriage and divorce announcements. I've even read the obituaries."

"Obituaries..." Ling says slowly.

"It means death notices," I explain.

"I know what it means..." Ling closes her eyes. "There was an obituary... The letter writer told Ma... Oh, that was when she began crying herself to sleep... Sir had died on board the ship."

"Your father? Died on the way back to England?" On the newspaper archive site, I'm already adjusting the search to: obituary, doctor William, 1918–25.

0 *results found for 'doctor William'*, it says in black letters on the screen.

When I remove 'doctor', a list of eighty-nine obituaries appear. We skim through them together, until Ling gasps and points at my screen.

I read the whole obituary aloud:

MALAYA TRIBUNE, 14TH JULY 1922, OBITUARY

We have to report with regret that long-term resident of the colony, Commanding Officer Mr William Thomas Davidson, who was a passenger on the SS Nellore, bound for Home, died on board and was buried at sea. Death was due to malaria complicated with toxic jaundice. Davidson began his career in the Royal Navy as a telegraphist in 1899, and rose in the ranks in service of the colonial administration. The telegram, received by the Singapore agent of the P and O company, further states that the late Mr Davidson's son, William Henry, as well as his second wife, Mrs Margaret Davidson, and her daughter, Violet, are proceeding to London.

"He was a telegraphist." I smack my hand against my forehead. "That's how you and William learnt Morse code! That's how you knew the old maritime distress signal."

There's no mention of Ling, but I don't think she had expected that. For some reason, she's crying. It's as if she's only now received news of her father's death.

Then my computer pings. It's a message from Granny. I read it twice before I call Ling out of her sorrow.

"Listen to this... Granny writes, 'Wilhelmina's maiden name was Davidson'."

I pause for effect, but Ling goes on crying.

"Isn't that amazing, Ling? It means we *are* related. You're my great-great-grand-aunt, or something like that. And tonight Granny will have a more thorough look through the box, so Dad can bring back whatever she discovers. She's already found a photo of Wilhelmina, holding my granddad, standing between her mother and father—your brother."

We've solved the mystery with a couple of days to spare. I feel like dancing around. It takes a while before I realize Ling isn't happy.

"What's wrong?"

"If William had died on the ship—my brother William—then that would explain why he did not come back for me." She sobs.

"But don't you see... If he'd died when he was a child, then he wouldn't have had children, and we couldn't have been related."

She shrugs, as if she doesn't care about that. "William promised he would never forget me, but he did. And he grew old enough to have a grandson."

"Maybe he didn't forget. We can't know that. We only have the facts."

Unfortunately, a key fact is that Ling died as a pauper among strangers.

"Maybe he didn't want to forget," I say, trying to cheer her up. "Maybe he locked all the memories of you away in a safe place, and then he lost the key."

— 39 —

On Friday night, I go to bed early, after telling Clementine I have a headache. It's not even a lie. I didn't fall asleep until after two o'clock last night. No matter what I said, I couldn't cheer Ling up. And Kiera's been badgering me all day. She's more annoyed with me for getting grounded than she is with Clementine. For fear Clementine would allow me to go, I haven't even told her about the sleepover.

Pools of rain slide down my window. In the next room, Clementine's reading to the twins. Their giggles sound through the wall.

It's the last night Ling's here. She's lying next to me on the bed. We're both miserable. After tomorrow evening, she'll be gone. I hope to a better place. I hope what we have discovered will be enough to ensure she isn't hungry any more. But I doubt it. She still isn't satisfied.

My last hope is that Granny will find proof that William didn't forget Ling. If only he'd done something like calling his own daughter Ling, but he didn't. Granny's already answered my email: Wilhelmina didn't have any middle names. Without asking questions, she's promised to search for anything related to Wilhelmina's father.

I have a nagging feeling we ought to return to the banyan tree and set the mythical creatures free. The first time we visited, Ling said it was the beginning, when the universe was in balance. But we left that world in chaos. Perhaps setting things right could help Ling. I haven't asked her what she thinks. Ten wild horses couldn't drag me there—as Aunt Astrid would say. I doubt even ten azure dragons could make me go back.

After two hours, I'm still not sleepy, so I sneak downstairs to fetch a glass of milk.

On the way to the kitchen, a lizard crosses my path and scurries under the dining table. It might be Lizzie—I haven't seen her today. Even if it isn't her, I have to save the creature from the glue traps behind the curtains.

Lying on my stomach, I push myself forward on the cool marble floor under the dining chairs. "Come on, Lizzie," I whisper, holding my cupped hands in front of me. "Before *she* sees you."

The lizard, which is bigger than Lizzie, quivers less than an arm's length away, when Clementine comes through the swing door from the kitchen with a cup of tea.

She's on the phone, saying, "Will believes she just needs to find her role in our family and then all will be well. But, frankly, I'm getting desperate." She sinks down on a sofa. "I remember you telling me about the problems with your stepson."

I don't think Clementine's told Dad about our fight, because he hasn't called, but she's telling her friends. She's probably posted a *Help!-My-husband's-daughter-is-impossible* message online.

"Thanks. I'm worried sick. Last week she claimed she saw a girl in our garden—which is fenced—and now she disappears to a local cemetery and god-knows-where without telling anyone. She ignores the twins, and I'm honestly afraid—"

The murmur coming from Clementine's phone is inaudible. What's she afraid of? I'm lying completely still, willing the lizard not to move.

"I told you about the tragedy, didn't I?"

My body trembles, and the lizard takes off, vanishing under the kitchen swing door.

"I can't even imagine... Will still has nightmares about it. Freja was six when it happened. She stopped talking for months, until she invented an imaginary friend to help her cope with the loss of—"

A loud wail from the twin's room interrupts Clementine. While she's walking upstairs, she tells her friend she'll call back later.

But I almost can't hear her for the rushing, peeping noise in my ears. It's the sound of a storm which has found a broken window and a gap by an ill-fitting door. The trapdoor to a loft. The gale blasts the trapdoor off its hinges. Air roars through the loft, blowing the cobwebs on the hidden box out of the window amid shards of glass. Before I can react, I catch a glimpse of the next animal letter: a monkey *M*.

Like the alligator, it's sketched in pencil. The monkey's lips are pulled back in a teeth-showing, joyless grin. Next to the monkey, a chain with an old-fashioned padlock encircles the box. There are two letters on the other side of the chain, but they're smudged. My vision blurs. The monkey grins at me. It jumps back and forth over the chain until I see two monkeys. As if the first monkey has a twin.

—40—

I run upstairs, while Clementine's still with Billy and Eddie. Inside my room, I lean against the closed door. I'm gasping and can't stop trembling.

"What is wrong?" Ling sits up on the bed.

"It's all wrong!" I try to force my shallow breathing to slow. I expected everything would be fine when we had solved the mystery of Ling's past, but it isn't. The mysterious box won't leave me alone.

"It is not all wrong. I am happy you helped me remember," Ling says. "I know you will not forget me. Perhaps now that I remember her, I can find Ma."

"That's good, Ling," I say without really listening to her.

"Come and sit here. I will tell you a story the Malay cook told me. I'm sorry I was not happy. We should chill this last night."

"No. We can't 'chill'. You've watched too much telly on my laptop. Everything's out of kilter. We have to free the myth-ical creatures. We have to put that world back in balance."

Afterwards, I might be able to forget about the box. Or perhaps I'll find a key to unlock the padlocked chain. "Tonight's our last chance. And I think there's something—something terrible—I ought to remember."

Ling studies me, with a concerned frown. "Then we must go," she says.

After getting dressed, I check my pockets. I have my compass, map, pen, paper, matches and first-aid kit. No phone, no knife. In the desk drawer, at the very back, I find my old Swiss Army knife. I got it when I was six. It's a kiddie knife with a blunt, rounded blade. The only pointed tool is the corkscrew, but it makes me feel slightly better prepared.

When I reach up to grasp the rope outside my window, the sky rumbles. Lit up by a flash of lightning, Ling floats to the ground, like a falling star.

By the time we pass Jason's house, I'm already drenched. The curtains in his bedroom upstairs twitch. The window opens, and he calls for me to stop.

Two minutes later he's standing inside the metal gate, under an umbrella. "Where're you going?" he wheezes. "It's late."

I point up towards the cemetery.

"You shouldn't be going up there. Aren't you grounded?"

I shrug. "It's okay. I'm with Ling." I walk away to catch up with her.

"But it's dark," he calls after me.

"I'm not *pantang*," I call back.

On the expressway, cars pass with loud swooshes, spraying water up in the air from deep pools on the road. Flickering blinks from the sky light up the beginning of the path into the rainforest. I know it's dangerous to go into a forest in a thunderstorm, but, this time, that doesn't stop me.

No matter how much I try, I can't remember any tragedy. Only all the sorrow.

Ling leads me through the darkness to the banyan tree and pulls me into a run. We're spinning and swirling, until we arrive out of breath in that other world.

My clothes are dry again, but I have no doubt they'll become soaked within minutes of leaving the banyan tree. The dragon's still circling in the haze above the smouldering forest. Rain's still pouring down outside, but at least the wind has died down.

We go directly to the pit, although I have no idea how to get the mythical creatures out of such a deep hole. I wish I'd brought a climbing pulley.

While I'm surveying the area, hoping something sparks an idea, I can't help wondering where Pontiana is, and whether she's the one who's captured the animals. We haven't seen any other human-like creatures here... no one else who could have made a net of lianas. But why?

"Why would Pontiana capture the tortoise and the tiger?" I ask out loud. "I understand if she caught the bird to save her baby—"

"Oh no." Ling's eyes open wide in an expression of utter horror.

I take hold of her shoulders to stop her shaking. "What's wrong? Can you see the baby anywhere?" Scanning the pit, I try to spot Pontiana or her baby hidden in the mud behind the giant tortoise.

"Oh, I should have realized..." Ling wrings her hands. "The banana grove, the scent of night flowers, her beauty, the crying baby..."

"What about the baby?"

"There is no baby, Freja. It was her. That is one of the things they do to attract prey. They cry like babies. When the sound is loud, they are far away. When it is quiet, they are nearby. That is exactly how it was. We thought the baby had been carried off, immediately before she appeared."

"I haven't a clue what you're on about. Can you just breathe and explain?"

"I know who she is: Pontiana. Cook told me stories about her. Horrible stories. I remember them now." Ling takes a ragged breath. "She is a *pontianak*."

"A *pontianak*? You mean, a vampire ghost?" So what, I almost ask. Ling's a ghost herself, and we're surrounded by strange creatures. Pontiana didn't harm us. "What's she going to do? Drink our blood? Eat us?"

"Only our organs. Well, yours. I am a ghost."

I shake my head. I remember the warm feeling inside when she smiled at me and I almost believed she was Mum. "But she was nice to us."

"Last time, she needed our help. If we free the mythical creatures, and she is the one who caught them, she will want revenge. We have to get away from here."

"But what about the animals?"

The white tiger growls, as if it understands we're talking about them.

"The four mythical creatures have existed since the beginning of time, how can a *pontianak* harm them?" Ling asks.

"You're not making sense, Ling. Someone captured them, right? If Pontiana really is a *pontianak*, isn't there a way to defeat her?"

Ling puts a finger into the dip between her collarbones, saying, "Cook claimed that a nail has to be hammered into a *pontianak*, right here."

"That's brutal! What if she isn't a *pontianak*? If we puncture a main artery, she could die."

"She is already dead, Freja."

Pontiana clearly isn't human, but still... "Well, it's no use, because we don't have any nails."

"What about your penknife?"

"This one?" I show her the short, blunt blade of my kiddie knife. "Clementine's confiscated my new knife. I could sharpen a wooden splinter, but that's probably not going to help much against your scary vampire ghost."

Ling shakes her head. "A *pontianak* is no joke."

"Then let's hurry and free the animals before Pontiana returns. We'll need the dragon to help us lift the tiger and the tortoise, but he doesn't like the vermillion bird. It might be best if I disentangle her first."

One of the banyan tree's branches reaches out above the pit. If I tie lianas together to make a rope, I can climb down from the branch. Although, going down into a confined space with an angry tiger—even if it's a mythical creature—might not be the best idea. But what else can we do?

I've just taken the knife out of my pocket to cut off a hanging root when I smell frangipani flowers.

"There you are, my dears." Pontiana strolls towards us, through the light rain. Her pristine white dress flows around her. She smiles, like she's missed us. And it's impossible to believe Ling's mad theory that she's a bloodthirsty, vengeful vampire ghost.

"Thank you so much for persuading the dragon. He should be finished soon. You did tell him to come here afterwards?"

Above the steam rising from the blackened forest, azure swirls encircle the darkest cloud.

I nod. "Where's your baby?" I ask.

"My baby..." Pontiana hesitates and frowns. "My baby is sleeping... inside the banyan tree."

That's a bit odd, as we didn't see a baby inside the den, but perhaps she put it down immediately before coming here. "I'm glad you caught the bird and saved your baby. Aren't you, Ling?"

"Yes," Ling mutters. She's standing rigidly by my side.

"Did you catch the tiger and the tortoise too?" I don't know what they have done to her, but the dragon is kind and helpful and I fear she might've set a trap for him.

"Nasty beasts," Pontiana hisses. "They want me to remember every single tortured moment."

Ling gasps.

As if she realizes something has changed, Pontiana glares at Ling with narrowed eyes. She puts her hands together and holds them up to her chin. The talons of her forefingers touch her red lips. I suddenly remember her nails stroking me and the drop of blood on my fingers. I raise a hand to my cheek. The three parallel scratches faded days ago, but it feels like they're burning. I shiver. Could Ling be right?

Pontiana catches me staring at her hands.

"Did you really capture those nasty beasts all by yourself?" I ask, trying to divert her attention. "That's amazing!" I twist my mouth into a grin. It's lucky that I'm a good liar.

Behind my back, I release the corkscrew on the knife in my hand. I hold it hidden in my fist, with the tool sticking out between two fingers. It's too short. It'll never work.

She comes so close, I'm enveloped in her peachy scent.

"You are a sweet girl," she says. "Exactly what I need." When she strokes my cheek with those sharp nails, it takes an immense effort not to flinch.

But then she gazes at me with Mum's grey-green eyes, and I can't believe she's bad. I just want her to hold me tight.

I forget what I'd planned, and say, "I miss my mum."

Pontiana giggles softly and puts her arms around me. Closing my eyes and inhaling her cloying scent, I relax into the embrace. Something melts inside me. Ling must be wrong.

"Freja!" Ling shrieks.

Pontiana's giggles become shrilly cackles. A stench of rotten meat surrounds me. I gag. When I look up, Pontiana's eyes have turned red.

She holds me in outstretched arms, gripping my shoulders so hard her nails are boring into my flesh. Her open mouth, full of pointed canine teeth, gapes. Her dress is in tatters, splattered with blood. There's absolutely nothing human about her.

At the same time as she swivels me sideways, she pulls one of her claw-like hands back, letting go of my right shoulder. It happens so fast; my reaction is a reflex. Before she can plunge her talons into my stomach, I thrust the corkscrew into the soft hollow in her neck.

The transformation is immediate. Pontiana shrinks until she isn't much taller than me. Her hair loses its shine and her skin darkens to light brown. She's still pretty, but she seems exhausted.

"I did not mean to harm the creatures." Tears run down Pontiana's cheeks and over her chapped lips. Her coarse, grey dress is tight over her round belly. She holds her hands as if they're cradling an unborn child. "I could not bear to think about my baby any more. I wanted to forget. I hoped if I upset the balance, all the world would disappear in oblivion."

"Shhh..." I press my hand against the red handle of the knife, so it doesn't fall out. Together, Ling and I guide Pontiana up into the banyan tree. I want both of them out of the way.

"Don't let go of the knife! She might become a *pontianak* again, if you do," I tell Ling, before I go back outside to wait.

When the azure dragon arrives, he hovers above the pit. His serpentine body rolls like endless waves, while I tell him my plan.

Afterwards, the dragon twists up a thunderstorm above the banyan tree. With precision, lighting strikes the tree exactly where the branch over the pit is attached to the trunk. The clap of thunder is still ringing in my ears, when there's a creak and the branch tumbles down. It hits the ground with a thump. Earth rains into the pit from the wall where the thickest part of the branch lands. On the opposite side of the pit, twigs break off, popping like pine cones in a bonfire.

The end of the branch only reaches halfway down the hole, but it's enough for the white tiger. It leaps up onto the gangplank and climbs out of the pit. At the top, its head turns towards me. The pale-blue eyes blink once, before the tiger bounds off to the west.

Although I can hardly see anything through the rain, I tie a hanging root around the top of the branch, and clamber down the slippery bark. When I drop to the ground, my hiking boots sink into the mud. Near the far wall of the pit, the tortoise is nothing more than a dark shape. Next to me, the vermillion bird struggles against the tight net. It takes a while to calm it down and loosen the knots without a knife. By the time it flies away, the water has risen above my knees.

The black tortoise paddles towards me. Coiled around its shell three times, like a climbing rope, is a snake as thick as my thigh. The geometrical net of its black-brown skin almost makes it blend in with the shapes on the tortoise shell. Perhaps that's the reason I hadn't noticed it earlier. It's a python. A monstrous python.

The lowest part of the branch is out of reach, but my root rope hangs close by. I grab it and start climbing. The moment the tortoise floats below me, the python's head lifts from the shell. Higher and higher it rises, matching my speed, right next to the rope.

It's not venomous, I tell myself. It might bite, though, or strangle me. I stop moving, clutching the root rope, and hold my breath.

The snake sways. Its mouth gapes, revealing a hundred sharp, back-turned teeth. The forked tongue flickers out. It licks the back of my hand. Then the snake drops back onto the shell of the tortoise.

I scramble up the rope, while watching them drift in the rising water.

When the pit is full, the rain stops. The black tortoise, with its rider, climbs out and lumbers towards the north of the island. At the bottom of the hill, they vanish between the naked, charred trees.

I turn towards the banyan tree where the azure dragon hovers. After I rub his ears in farewell, he flies east.

The four mythical creatures have returned to their own corners of the world.

—42—

I close my eyes and take a deep breath. The bonfire-smoke scent from the charred wound where the lighting struck the tree calms me. But only for a second. In my mind, one of the two monkeys unlocks the memory box. With unchanged, unhappy grins, the monkeys start dancing to trumpet music, while the alligator taps out a rhythm with its sharp teeth.

"What now?" I ask Ling, shaking my head to get rid of the bizarre image. "We can't take her with us back to Bukit Brown."

Next to Ling, Pontiana sits slumped against the trunk. She might be sleeping. Below Ling's hand, my knife handle is still sticking out from her neck.

"We must bring her back to the realm of the dead. The Hell Guards will make sure she does not escape."

I shudder at the memory of the statues I saw at Har Paw Villa.

While I hold the handle of the knife in place, we drag

216

Pontiana to her feet. We each take one of her hands, before we start running.

The spinning stops when I touch one of the golden handles. The moment the towering gates open to the thundercloud greyness, I hear the crying child.

"Goodbye," Ling says, as we shove Pontiana inside.

Pontiana clings to my arm, pleading to come with us. I want to extract my knife and don't even think about what might happen when she becomes a *pontianak* again, but it's stuck. Turning the corkscrew, I get the knife free. Pontiana's nails grow and bite into my wrist.

I'm trying to prise her talons off my arm, when she stumbles. She falls, pulling me with her. The knife slips out of my grip. I land on hands and knees next to Pontiana.

She shrieks and scrambles away from me. While I search for my knife, I struggle to get up. But it's as if gravity has changed. I'm weighed down by a thousand stones.

After giving up finding the knife, I finally manage to stand. That's when I discover that I'm inside the gates.

Pontiana has pulled me into the realm of the dead.

The child cries again. It doesn't sound like Pontiana's baby; this one's older. There are real words in its wailing babble. It must be scared.

I want to find it. Help it. Hold it tight.

The flaps on the memory box lift.

I can't move my feet. A grey, swirling, mumbling mass flows past me, tugging at me like a river before a waterfall. If it wasn't for the thousand stones weighing me down, I couldn't stay standing. In slow-motion, I raise a heavy arm towards Ling.

"Help me," I yell.

Ling holds on to one of the golden door handles and stretches her other hand towards me, but I'm too far away.

Behind me, the child wails louder. I can understand what it's saying. It keeps repeating the same syllable: "Fei-fei, Fei-fei."

"You must want to remember," Ling shouts.

And I do.

And I remember.

All this time, there have been two forgotten lives. One Ling wanted to remember and one I wanted to forget.

Light floods my memory loft. I can see the animal letters clearly. An elephant, twin monkeys and the gloomy alligator. Images float out of the open box. Like early morning mist rising from a swamp, they glimmer in and out of focus. In every one of them, a little girl with yellow flyaway hair reaches her arms towards me, calling, "Fei-fei."

I know exactly who she is. And I know I can't leave her here alone.

I give up fighting the grey river. It carries me to the precipice of a waterfall.

Far below, the little girl's crying. She needs me. I can stay here with her, if I leap.

But before I jump, a hand closes around my wrist. I twist to escape Ling's grip, but she holds on tight.

"Remembering is enough!" Ling yanks at my arm and shouts my name.

There's another noise, like rusty bells chiming. It's blocking the cries. Ling's hair brushes against my cheek and covers my eyes, hindering my view of the little girl.

I realize Ling's right. Now, that I remember, I can bring the little girl with me. She will always live on in my memories and in my heart.

And I can't stay in here. I have to get back to Mum and Dad and Clementine and Billy and Eddie. They need me, too.

"Come on, Freja!" Ling says. Somewhere far away, outside the gates, a whole chorus echoes Ling, calling my name.

Together, we fight a current that's neither water nor wind back towards the gates. Here two figures loom above us, blocking the exit with their spears. The Hell Guards: Ox-head and Horse-face. They resemble the Haw Par Villa statues as much as an attacking lion resembles a sleepy kitten.

"You cannot pass," they say with one voice.

"It is not the end of the festival yet," Ling argues.

All around us, spirits murmur. We spin through layers of time and space in complete darkness. There are no stars. Then a white-hot brightness tears us apart, and I'm falling.

And falling.

My ears are ringing with the sound of clanking keys.

But I remember Emma.

"F reja! Freja!"

The round yellow brightness of a torch is bouncing towards me, accompanied by a rhythmic jangle of keys.

"I'm here, Jason." I try to get up, but I can't. Something's holding me down. "Ling!" I call.

"*Aiyoh!*" Jason blinds me with his lamp, before he sweeps it around and up and down. "The tree must've been hit by lightning. Are you okay?"

"Yeah." I look around, trying to spot Ling. "Ling! Where are you?"

"Who's Ling?" someone asks. It sounds like Sunitha. What's she doing here?

Jason throws light on the trunk and the scorched, ragged area where the branch used to be. It has stopped raining. The normal sounds of the rainforest have returned.

"Oh my goodness," Kiera squeals. "You're sooo lucky that didn't land on you or you'd be flat as a waffle."

The branch is right next to my legs, which are tangled

into a web of hanging roots. I tear at them to get free, stopping midway to check the pockets of my soaked pants for my knife. It isn't there.

"What are you doing here?" Sunitha asks.

"In a graveyard. At night. During the seventh month?" Cheryl Yi continues. She jangles a bunch of keys even bigger than Jason's.

"What happened? Why were you just lying there?" Jason asks. The flashlight makes it impossible to see any of their faces.

"I fell down. Can you see my knife anywhere? It's red." I don't need it to cut through the roots, because I've untangled the last one from the laces of my soaked hiking boots. Even my socks are wet. But I can't remember if I picked the knife up after I dropped it or not.

The beam from Jason's torch is shining on the ground, drawing spirals around me, while I'm tying my bootlaces.

Suddenly, Sunitha yells, "Snake! Freja, get away from there."

Jason shrieks as loudly as the three girls. His light beam shakes on the fallen branch.

Like a crab, I scramble backwards, away from the danger. "Hold the torch still, Jason. I need to check what it is," I say when I'm standing.

For one long moment, I'm worried. Snake venom can cause hallucinations. What if my visit to the underworld was just that? A feverish dream. But already before I see the snake, I know that isn't the case, because I remember every little detail. Even the memories I'd locked away.

The snake is curled around the branch and rolled up like a monster cinnamon bun. It appears to be fast asleep.

"It's only a python," I say. "They're not venomous."

"I know, it's a constrictor." Jason backs further away. "But it's massive!"

"It's like... It's sooo... I don't even..."

"As thick as Jason's upper arm," Sunitha says, while Kiera for once is speechless.

"And pythons have teeth." Jason adds.

"I know," I say. I want to tell them I've seen the teeth up close and that this one isn't massive, but I don't. "My knife might be up by the trunk. Can I borrow your torch, Jason?"

Jason goes with me, throwing the light where I tell him, into the cage around the trunk. "There's probably snakes in here too," he mumbles.

The girls are right behind us. None of them want to stay near the python. They're badgering me to get out the graveyard.

"Just give me five minutes."

Like a scout patrol with me as the leader, we walk in single file around the trunk inside the ring of banyan tree roots.

"Cool hidey-hole," Kiera says, "There's just one problem: location, location, location."

"Completely agree." Jason nods so much the light beam see-saws.

I kick dead leaves aside and scrape debris out of gaps between roots with a stick, until the others persuade me to give up. The knife's gone. For ever.

"Thank you, kiddie knife," I whisper under my breath.

Without speaking, we make our way down to the asphalt pathway. From there, the three girls walk in front, with Kiera swinging the torch and Cheryl Yi jangling her keys. Kiera and Sunitha are chatting as if they were out on a normal daytime walk, and not a midnight hike. They're all wearing flip-flops, which isn't ideal. And pyjamas, I notice, that at least are long and cover their legs and arms.

"What happened?" Jason whispers. "Where's Ling?"

"I don't know. I hope she's waiting for me at home."

"And your knife?" he asks.

"I used it to vanquish a *pontianak*."

"Don't joke about *pontianak*s!" Jason jangles his keys furiously, then glances sideways at me and says, "You're not joking, are you?"

We stop outside his house. In the glow from the tea lights on the offering plates, both Cheryl Yi and Kiera stare at me.

"Gosh, you look like you've been dragged through the mud." Kiera starts picking leaves and twigs out of my wet hair. I must've set a new grubbiness record. My clothes are soaked. My trousers are caked in mud up to my knees, and my T-shirt up to the elbows.

"How come you're actually here?" I ask the girls. "Did Jason call you?"

"No, no." Sunitha titters. "We were at Kiera's house and—"

"We thought you'd be lonely as a church mouse," Kiera interrupts. "And perhaps we could persuade your wicked stepmother to let you come over, so we sneaked out. To distract Mum, I told Cillian that Liam had eaten the whole tub of ice cream. Big brothers can be quite useful..."

"But when we got there, Jason was lurking around your house, trying to peep through the fence." Sunitha raises one eyebrow and winks at me.

"I wanted to make sure she'd made it back home okay. I was worried, okay!"

"I'd be worried, too," Cheryl Yi says.

"Anyway, your day-curtains were fluttering outside the window and the rope hanging down. You said you always hid it after using it, so I guessed you still weren't home. And then they came walking down the street... in their... pyjamas..." Jason waves a hand at the three girls.

"Jason told us where're you'd gone." Cheryl Yi shakes her head.

"I knew I'd never find the gravestone, but I remembered the big tomb with the ant-covered offerings, and I thought I might be able to find the banyan tree."

Sunitha smiles. "And, of course, we wanted to help find you, because—"

"A friend in need is a friend in deep. And look at you..." Kiera gives me another up-down-up scan. "You were obviously in really deep water."

Outside the dark house, we all hug, even though I'm so filthy. I hug Jason and Cheryl Yi extra hard, because I understand how scared they must've been. I don't want to think about what would've happened if my friends hadn't found me. If they hadn't called me back from the realm of the dead.

When I come out of a long shower, Ling's sitting on my window seat. It's after midnight. The last day of the Hungry Ghost Festival has begun.

Ling says she isn't sure exactly when she'll be forced to end her holiday, but she needs to feed on some offerings first. She promises to stay until I've fallen asleep.

I promise to remember her and come back to Singapore next year during the seventh month.

None of us mention the underworld. She doesn't ask me what I remembered inside the gates. And I'm afraid to ask if she'll have to return there. Instead, I try to replace my memory of that horrible place with an image of Ling and her mother together on a fluffy cloud.

We say goodbye, just in case. Afterwards, we lie in silence, turned towards each other on my bed, her hand covering mine like a little cooling cloud.

I want to tell her about Emma, but I can't find the words. Because how can I explain to Ling that, just like her brother, I'd forgotten my little sister?

−44−

It's early morning, and the house is quiet when I sneak downstairs. Before anyone wakes up, I want to hose down my clothes and hiking boots in the garden. Last night, I left everything among the branches of the tree, and climbed up to my room in my vest and knickers.

The bottom stair creaks.

"Is that you, Maya?" Clementine calls from the office.

"No, it's me," I answer. The garden hose will have to wait.

Clementine's sitting on the floor, dressed in yoga clothes, surrounded by stacks of books. She lifts more out of a shopping bag and places them on a pile of picture books. There are stacks with books for older children and a tumbled heap of paperbacks with crinkled covers, for grown-ups.

"What're all those books for?" I ask. Behind her are at least ten full paper bags.

"My project," she says, continuing to sort. "These are the English books people here in Singapore have donated.

Obviously, I'll be buying books in Khmer when I go to Cambodia in two weeks. Can you believe we raised more than twenty thousand dollars at the event last week? After I've paid for the building materials, that still leaves a lot of money for books."

"But *who* are they for?"

"One moment, Freja. I just need to post an update." With her phone held close to the floor, so the stacks appear to be mountains, she takes a short video clip. While typing, she mumbles, "Thank you for the generous book donations to our new libraries in Cambodia. Keep them coming! Please share this post." She copies both video and message onto her different profiles.

I'm not sure what I imagined she was posting online, but not this.

"Come here and bring my laptop. It's on the desk. Then I'll show you what it's all about," she says.

When I'm sitting next to her, while she's searching for photos, she starts telling me about her charity organization and the libraries they're building in rural Cambodia.

"Ah, here we go. These are from the library we built in Kampong Khleang in March."

I'm silent while she flips through the photos. They show a group of women who literally are building a library, which is a shack made of corrugated iron on high wooden stilts. Clementine's standing on a ladder, wearing grimy clothes and protective gloves, hammering nails into a green plate.

The library resembles many of the houses around it. Some have walls of straw, but they're all on raised platforms. The packed dirt underneath them is littered with plastic and rubbish.

"They have terrible floods in the rainy season," Clementine says to explain the stilts.

In another photo, barefooted children in grubby vests and shorts flock around Clementine. She crouches, a black chicken pecking at her hiking boot, while she hands out books.

I peek sideways at Clementine. She really is a completely different person than I thought.

"So... when we were at that restaurant with the sponsor..." I say, beginning to understand why it was so important for her.

"He made generous donations to our auction." She's smiling that big, happy, lipstick smile. "What's up with you, Freja?"

I stare down at a picture book with a happy family on the cover.

"I understand if you're having a difficult time. And I want you to know that I'm here for you. I know I'm not your mum, and I'm not trying to take her place, but I would love to play a bigger part in your life. As a stepmother—a third parent—or a friend. It's up to you."

There's also a dog on the picture book. It's wagging its tail. I'm sure there aren't any stepmothers in this story. But if there was one, she would be a cheerful person, like Clementine.

"A real friend."

"I have real friends," I say quietly. For the first time in for ever, I have real friends: Kiera and Sunitha and Cheryl Yi and Jason.

"That's great. I'm so happy for you. Then..." she hesitates. "Then you don't need imaginary friends. We're so worried about you, Freja."

"You really don't have to be. I don't have a new imaginary friend..." The worst thing that can happen is that she laughs at me and thinks I have too much imagination. "Ling isn't imaginary. She's a hungry ghost... a dead relative we've all forgotten about... Do you think that's ridiculous?"

Clementine isn't laughing. "No. Don't forget I grew up in Hong Kong, where the aunties warned me about being outside at night during the seventh month. Tell me about this ghost."

"We've discovered that she's my great-great-grandfather's little sister. Half-sister. And she was left here when the family moved back to England in 1922. She believes everyone forgot her. That's why she's so unhappy. If I could just find proof that someone remembered her..."

"What was your great-great-great-grandfather's name?" Clementine asks.

"William Thomas Davidson. But he died. I even have a photo of the obituary."

"Where? On your phone?" She gets up and retrieves my phone from a drawer.

It should've synchronized from my laptop. On the locked screen, there's a message from Granny.

I found a memoir by William Henry. Your dad is bringing it back to Singapore.

I show both the message and the obituary to Clementine.

"Hmm... I think I might've seen that memoir when we moved in..." She gets up and stands by the bookcase, scanning the titles. "It's called something like '*Singapore and the Colonies*'..."

I spot it first. *A Life in the Colonies—from Singapore to The West Indies* by William Henry Davidson. There's a painting of a bungalow on the front cover. A black-and-white in a tropical garden.

After Clementine has brought us cushions from one of the white sofas, we lie down between the stacks on the floor, our heads close together, and turn the pages. We're both reading, and whenever one of us notices something that might be relevant, we add a sticky-note and read aloud to the other.

Clementine skips her yoga class and asks Maya to entertain the boys and bring us a plate of sandwiches. When we're done, a fan of sticky notes juts out of the book.

Afterwards, we lie on our backs and talk about Ling and William. It's nice to lie here with Clementine. I like that she believed me. I like that she helped me find and read the book. I like her. And it's okay to like her. That doesn't mean she'll ever replace Mum.

—45—

I hike up to the cemetery late in the afternoon. Dad will be landing soon. Clementine has been out to buy me joss sticks and hell banknotes. She even offered to come with me, but I told both her, and later Jason, that I had to do this on my own. I'm crossing my fingers so hard they hurt, hoping I'll find Ling before it's too late.

My Swiss Army knife—the new one—is in my pocket, and I'm using the map on my phone to find the grove. I slosh up to the rainforest in my soaked hiking boots.

After I've placed an offering plate on the gravestone, I stick burning joss sticks into a thick pumpkin slice. Next to it, I place a bundle of the paper money and light it with a match. I sit upwind of the fire and wait.

When the air cools and the cicada noise mutes, the flames flicker.

Ling appears. She stands on the other side of the gravestone. Tendrils of smoke curl around her hair and her long neck.

"William never forgot you, Ling. This book is proof. He wrote it. Look!" I hold the memoir towards her, so she can see his name and the house on the cover. "He mentions you so many times. Do you want me to read to you?"

She's listening, while I read snippets to her about William's childhood.

"When I was almost four, my *amah* gave birth to a girl. Ling. From the first time I laid eyes on her, I adored her, long before I discovered she was my half-sister. I can only imagine the scandal a child of a Chinese nursemaid and a British officer would have caused at the time. Still, I wish my father had had the courage to acknowledge Ling as his daughter.

"It was a happy childhood, in that black-and-white bungalow at the edge of the rainforest. After school, I played with Ling in the garden, and taught her to read and write both English and our father's secret 'dot-dash language', as Ling called Morse code.

"After the admiral's wife persuaded my father to marry the widow of another officer, everything changed. When my stepmother discovered the truth about Ling, she dismissed her mother and only kept Ling on as a kitchen maid to appease me and the cook. By then my father was so ill with malaria that he could not intervene. In the hopes of restoring his health, we travelled by ship home to England."

I gaze across at Ling.

"We already know what happened on board that ship. In England, William was sent to boarding school. He ran away

232

to sea before he was supposed to start university." I flip to the next sticky-note and hold the text towards her.

"On this page, he describes how he searched for you, going door-to-door through Chinatown, asking if anyone knew what had happened to you or your mother. But that was in 1928, and you had both been dead for years by then."

I tell her the gist of the places marked by the next few sticky-notes. How throughout his years with the foreign office, her brother continued his search in archives and whenever his travels took him to Singapore.

The last chapter of William's memoir ends with:

My sole regret is that I was forced to leave Ling behind, and never during my later enquiries discovered what had become of her after we left the colony. My deepest hope is that she married a good man, changed her name and led a long, happy life with healthy children.

I close the book. "So, you see, Ling, even if no one made offerings, you were never forgotten."

Ling's crying. I don't try to stop her. She's smiling at the same time.

When I take the paper school bag out, she smiles even wider. "D'you like it?"

She nods. With its red and yellow swirly pattern, it's almost too pretty to burn. But that's the only way she can take it with her: like a smoke memory.

Ling inhales the school bag fumes. "Now that I know William did not forget me, I am happy," she says. "Are you

233

happy, Freja? Will you tell me what you did not want to remember?"

"I had a little sister. Her name was Emma. She died." The last word grates in my throat. "It was that day, the day we stopped being a happy family, that I didn't want to remember."

Ling stretches her arm across the gravestone and touches my shoulder with her coolness.

"I was six. Emma was two, like the twins. It was summer. We were visiting my friend Christopher. Denise, my other best friend, was also there with her parents. The three of us ran around inside the house, chasing each other through the kitchen, where the mums were arranging salads. Outside on the terrace, the dads shooed us away from the hot barbecue. Christopher said he would show us his tree house. Emma toddled after us, but I said she couldn't come. I knew she couldn't climb the ladder."

Ling nods as if she knows too.

"I told her to find Mummy, that it was too dangerous for her. Before I followed my friends up into the tree house, I went back and pushed her towards the kitchen. I even pulled the ladder up after me so she wouldn't try to crawl up and fall down. For a while she stood below, calling, 'Fei-fei,' and crying. I yelled at her to go away, to leave me alone. I remember being so relieved when she finally toddled off." The fire flares when I feed it banknotes. "I'm sure William never told you to go away."

"If he did, I have forgotten," Ling says quietly.

"I never thought Emma wasn't with Mum. I didn't even think about the tiny pond behind the house, where

Christopher and I used to catch tadpoles. The water only came up to my knees." I study the dirty, worn patches, where my knees are now. They're much higher up than six-year-old knees. But not nearly as high as a two-year-old's head.

"We were sitting at the table, blowing bubbles with our straws, while the adults kept calling Emma's name. Then Mum screamed. I held my hands to my ears to block the too-loud sounds: Mum's screams, the ocean waves crashing in my head, the sirens of the ambulance. Blue light flooded the garden. The adults were crying. I was crying. The crying went on and on, for days and weeks and months. But all the tears in the world couldn't bring Emma back." I rub my eyes. They're itching.

"You locked the memory of that day away in a safe place," Ling says. "Without meaning to, you locked Emma away too. And then you lost the key."

"Thank you for helping me find the key." I try to smile. "I promise I won't lose it again. I'll always remember my little sister."

Ling's standing completely still, while a rush of cool air swirls around me, like a flutter of angel wings.

−46−

In the evening, I'm sitting on a blanket in the garden with Dad. A portable, bowl-shaped fireplace that Clementine's borrowed stands in front of us. On it, I've built a small pyramid of coal and twigs and pieces of wood from sticks I've found in Bukit Brown.

After I tell Dad about Ling and how she's related to us through my great-great-grandfather, he leafs through the memoir with all the sticky-notes. The photos he brought back from Granny are inside a well-used copy of the same book.

The second photo makes me gasp. On the back, in joined-up letters is written: William Henry, 1918. But the photo isn't only of William. He's sitting on the steps leading up to a veranda, next to a young Chinese woman with her hair in a tight bun. On his other side, a girl with long, dark hair stands, with her hand on his shoulder. Both children are smiling. Identical dimples, like little commas, make dents in their cheeks.

I hold the photo up to show it to Ling, and she comes and sits next to me. Dad doesn't notice.

"So, can we burn the money, Dad? Tonight's the last night of the Hungry Ghost Festival."

"You have a very lively imagination, Freja." He sighs. "I'm sorry I've been travelling so much. Now the Manila contracts are done, I promise I'll take some time off."

"It's not fantasy. Ling isn't imaginary. You needn't worry about me."

"I don't suppose it can harm to burn a bit of paper."

Although his attitude isn't quite right, I'm glad he's willing to make an effort. When the little bonfire's burning, I use it to light the joss sticks and push them into the ground in a large circle around us. I give him half of the bundle of money. He studies a banknote in the firelight.

"Hell Bank Note," he reads. "At least it's honest. Perhaps they should print it as a warning, on all currencies."

One by one, we feed the money to the fire and our hungry ghost. The edges of the notes glow, lighting up the colourful pictures of birds, before the paper money turns into nectar for Ling. Smoke with the right bonfire smell floats towards the frangipani trees, where Ling's dancing.

That was the easy part.

I suck in the smoky air and say, "I remember Emma. I remember the day she drowned."

Dad's eyes are deep pools with orange glints from the bonfire.

I'm glad he doesn't say anything, because it's hard enough to speak without him interrupting.

"I was supposed to look after her. But she couldn't climb up to the tree house—"

Dad grips my arm. "Never for one second believe that it

237

was your fault." He crushes me in a bearhug, and mumbles into my hair. "My little blue titmouse, of course it wasn't your fault. You were such a tiny thing yourself. It happened so fast. I never blamed anyone but myself. And your mum blames herself. But you... no one, *no one* ever blamed you."

There's a lump in my throat. "I yelled at Emma to leave me alone. It was the last thing I ever said to her."

Everything's blurry. My cheeks are wet. I don't remember tears being so salty.

Warm splashes land on my forehead. Dad's holding me tight. We're both shaking.

And I know that he's right. I was only six years old. It wasn't my fault. Blaming myself almost crushed me. It's what's crushing Mum, too. It isn't me. I'm not the reason she's sad. I'm not the reason our family wasn't happy.

"Te... tell me about Em... ma," I hiccup. "What was she li... like?"

Dad sniffs and lets go of me to wipe his face on the front of his T-shirt. "She was a wild little thing," he begins and encloses me in his arms again. "She worshipped you. Followed you like a shadow from the moment she could crawl—"

"Calling 'Fei-fei'," I interrupt.

"Ah yes. 'Fei-fei'. You were so patient with her. You played with her for hours, read her stories and had endless tea parties. Mum and I would lie on the sofa, exhausted, and watch how she giggled every time you pretended to drink from the miniature teacups."

Dad goes on talking, telling me little things about Emma, helping me remember. We sit there, holding each other, while I'm hearing echoes of Emma's giggles and seeing her shadow nearby.

I think about her and Ling. Two sisters. Both forgotten.

From now on, I'm going to remember both of them; grieve for both of them. They might be dead, but they will always be part of my life.

"Have you got a photo of Emma?" I ask, much later, when my eyes are only leaking.

Without a word, Dad pulls his phone out, opens a folder and lets me scroll through the pictures. Many of them are of both me and Emma. There are two photos I recognize, because I saw them in Dad's work office: the one of the kicking, smiling baby that I thought was me; and the one from the beach where I'm falling into Dad's arms and Mum looks so happy, sitting on a beach blanket next to a little girl with flyaway hair.

"Will Mum get better?"

"I believe so. Astrid says the treatment's working. None of us realized how much she needed help. I'm sorry about that, too."

The sliding glass door opens. Clementine is silhouetted against the light from the lounge. "Do you need anything? Something to drink perhaps?"

"Tissues," Dad says.

Clementine comes closer. She pulls a packet of Kleenex out of her pocket and throws it to Dad.

"Are the tw—Are Eddie and Billy still awake?" I ask.

"Maya's getting them ready for bed."

"Would it be okay if they came out here for a bit? Perhaps they can also burn some money. Or is that too dangerous?"

Dad frowns. "I'm not sure—"

"If you help them, Freja, they'll be fine." Clementine smiles.

Five minutes later, Billy and Eddie run across the lawn, calling, "Frej-ja." Instead of heading for Dad, they throw themselves at me.

"Careful!" I wrap my arms around them. "The fire's very hot."

When they're sitting next to me, I help them, one at a time, toss a paper one-dollar note into the flames.

"Where birdie gone?" Eddie asks when his note curls up.

I give him another.

"Here birdie!" He crumbles it in his sticky hand and holds it to his chest.

Billy's more interested in the photo that's lying in front of me.

"That's Ling." I let go of him to point at the little girl with her arms around another William. By the frangipani trees, Ling's still dancing in the smoke from her bonfire.

"Ling," Billy says and follows my gaze.

When Ling waves, he waves back.

Clasping the twins, I lean backwards until the three of us are lying on the blanket. Eddie snuggles into my arm, but Billy wiggles.

"Look!" I say and point at a spark from the bonfire.

Billy stops fidgeting. Eddie points his own little finger. Together we trace the twinkling fleck up, until it vanishes against the murky, yellowy sky.

I can't see the stars, but I know that they're there—an infinite number of lights in my expanding universe.

GLOSSARY

AIYOH Exclamation meaning "Oh no!" or "Oh dear!"

ALAMAK Exclamation used to express shock or surprise.

AH MA A Chinese word for grandmother.

AMAH A Chinese word for nanny or nursemaid.

ANG MO Singlish slang for a white person.

BERHATI-HATI DI RUANG PLATFORM "Mind the gap" in Malay.

BLUR LIKE SOTONG Literally means "blur like a squid". Singlish expression used to indicate that someone is clueless.

CHI (OR CH'I) Life force or energy flow, which plays an essential role in *feng shui*.

CHICKEN RICE A dish of poached chicken and seasoned rice, served with chilli sauce and cucumber garnishes.

CAN A one-word shortcut to saying, "Yes, I can" or "Can you do that?"

CANNOT A one-word shortcut to saying, "No, I can't" or "No, you can't."

CARROT CAKE A savoury omelette-like dish of steamed white radish that is fried with eggs, garlic and rice flour.

CATCH NO BALL Singlish expression that means to fail to understand something.

DON'T ANYHOW A phrase that means "Don't [do something] haphazardly" or "Don't [do something] willy-nilly".

DOSA A thin South-Indian pancake made from a fermented rice-based batter that is usually served with a lentil-based stew and chutney.

FENG SHUI A traditional practice originating from ancient China, which claims to use energy forces to harmonize individuals with their surrounding environment. Using *feng shui* principles, *yin* and *yang* are balanced to optimize *chi*.

GETAI Live stage performances held during the Hungry Ghost Festival to entertain both the living and the dead.

HAWKER CENTRE A market in which individual vendors sell a wide variety of inexpensive food.

HELL GUARDS Ox-head and Horse-face are the guardians of the realm of the dead in Chinese mythology. Both have the bodies of men, but Ox-head has the head of an ox while Horse-face has the head of a horse.

HUNGRY GHOST FESTIVAL A traditional Buddhist and Taoist festival held in the seventh month of the Chinese lunar calendar. During this month, ghosts—especially of those forgotten by their descendants—are on holiday from the realm of the dead and roam the streets to seek food and entertainment. The living make offerings of food and paper effigies to appease these roaming spirits.

JE SUIS "I am" in French.

KAMPONG A Malay word for village.

KIMZUA Literally means "gold paper", and includes the effigies and hell banknotes that are burnt as offerings to appease ghosts.

KUEH PIE TEE A tiny, thin and crispy pastry shell that is filled with a mixture of vegetables and shrimp.

LAH Singlish slang often used at the end of sentences to add emphasis.

LAST TIME Can mean any time in the past.

MOI "Me" in French.

MONKEY GOD Also known as Sun Wukong, a legendary hero—a monkey with superpowers, born from a magic stone—from the 16th-century Chinese novel *Journey to the West*.

MOON CAKES A Chinese cake eaten during the Mid-Autumn Festival, which takes place in the month following the Hungry Ghost Festival.

PANTANG To be superstitious.

PIGSY A fallen deity in the shape of a man with a pig's head, who is a companion of Monkey God in *Journey to the West*.

PONTIANAK A female vampiric ghost from South East Asian folklore.

POPIAH A thin paper-like pancake that is filled with a stew that typically includes turnip, bamboo shoots, lettuce, Chinese sausage, prawns, bean sprouts, garlic and peanut.

ROTI PRATA A South-Indian many-layered fried flatbread that is usually served with a curry.

SATAY Grilled meat skewers that are served with a sweet and spicy peanut sauce and cubes of compressed rice.

SKAT Term of endearment that means "treasure" in Danish.

SINGLISH A variety of English spoken in Singapore, incorporating elements of Chinese and Malay.

YIN Female, passive energy forces in the universe, according to Chinese philosophy.

YANG Male, active energy forces in the universe, according to Chinese philosophy.

WAH Exclamation used to express admiration.

WANTON MEE A dish of noodles, barbecued pork, leafy vegetables and dumplings that is served with a bowl of hot broth on the side.

WET MARKET A market selling fresh meat, fish, fruit and vegetables.

MORSE CODE ALPHABET

A	•—	U	••—
B	—•••	V	•••—
C	—•—•	W	•——
D	—••	X	—••—
E	•	Y	—•——
F	••—•	Z	——••
G	——•	Æ	•—•—
H	••••	Ø	———•
I	••	Å	•——•—
J	•———		
K	—•—	1	•————
L	•—••	2	••———
M	——	3	•••——
N	—•	4	••••—
O	———	5	•••••
P	•——•	6	—••••
Q	——•—	7	——•••
R	•—•	8	———••
S	•••	9	————•
T	—	0	—————

WORD SEPARATOR: /

SENTENCE SEPARATOR: //

```
-.. . .- .-./.-. . .- -.. . .-.//

- .... .. -. -.-/
-..- --- ..-/.... --- .-./
..-. . .- -.. .. -. --./- .... ./
.... ... -. --- .-- -.-./
--. .... --- ... -//
../.... --- .-.. ./-..- --- ..-/
. -. .--- --- -.-- . -../- ....
./
.- -.. .... . -. - ... ... .//
.... .- .... ./.... ... -./
--- .-. .. - .. -. --./
-- --- .-. ... ./
-- . ... ... .- --. . ...//

..../.../-. --- .-. ... .---//
```

ACKNOWLEDGEMENTS

I'm immensely grateful for all the stars in my universe—my friends and my extended family. Thanks to Marcus, August and Claus for their love and support, for our shared Singapore experiences and for their patience whenever I'm lost in my fictional worlds. And to my dad and my siblings, Dorte and Henrik, (all fellow veteran scouts) for always being there for me and for a childhood spent enjoying (or enduring) outdoor activities.

I'm eternally indebted to my brilliant editor, Sarah Odedina, for helping me shape this story through three very different incarnations of the plot. Sarah has been part of this journey from the initial idea, and I could not have written this book without her invaluable feedback in our discussions and at a memorable editorial meeting in Bukit Brown Cemetery in torrential rain. (You might have noticed our cameo in chapter fifteen.)

Heartfelt thanks to Tilda Johnson for making the text shine with her excellent line and copy edits, to Anna Morrison for designing yet another stunning cover, and to the fantastic team at Pushkin Press—I'm so proud my stories are part of the Pushkin family.

I owe an enormous debt of gratitude to Denise Tan, bookseller extraordinaire at Closetful of Books, for her early enthusiasm for this book and for sensitivity reading of the finished manuscript and correction of my Singlish expressions. Any remaining mistakes are entirely my own.

I would also like to thank the friends and writer friends in SCBWI Singapore, The Singapore Writers' MG & YA Group, SCBWI Switzerland and the Cafe Schreiber group, who helped this story on its way, especially: Jo Furniss, Felicia Low-Jimenez, David Liew, Dave Seow and Annette Woschek.

Massive thanks to readers, teachers, librarians, book bloggers, reviewers, booksellers and authors who have supported *The Missing Barbegazi*. It has been a joy to befriend so many wonderful people from the world of children's books, online or in real life. There are too many to name, but a few individual book champions must be mentioned, particularly Scott Evans and the PrimarySchoolBookClub, Louise (Book Murmuration), Naomi (Through the Looking Glass), Luna (Luna's Little Library) and Catherine (Story Snug). Being able to share successes (and concerns) with other children's authors is the best thing about social media, and I feel especially lucky to have connected with Sinéad O'Hart, Juliette Forrest, Victoria Williamson, Vashti Hardy and Piers Torday.

I will never forget our four amazing years in Singapore. Bukit Brown Cemetery is one of my favourite places on the island, but unlike Freja I also love the hustle and bustle of hawker centres and wet markets, Chinatown, Little India and the Arab Street quarter. I miss my morning walks in Botanic Gardens, late night strolls in Gardens by the Bay and hikes in MacRitchie. I miss the food, the MRT and the libraries. Most of all, I miss living in a cultural melting pot and, obviously, the wonderful people I met in Singapore.

Finally, thanks to the Bukit Brown Brownies, for gripping storytelling on their free guided tours of Bukit Brown Cemetery. I fervently hope this enchanting place will be conserved so future generations can discover some of its secrets and stories.